The GOOD GIRLS

The
GOOD GIRLS

Teresa Mummert

ISBN: 1508755132
ISBN 13: 9781508755135

www.TeresaMummert.com

SYNOPSIS

My life was meticulously planned, and I refused to deviate from that path. While my peers were partying, I prepared for the future. Then a tragic event destroyed everything, and I learned that while I was looking ahead, I forgot to live in the moment.

Starting over seemed impossible until I met Cara McCarthy, who lived every day like it was her last. She opened my eyes to a world of chaos and disorder. I loved every minute of it. She was also dating Tristan Adams, one of the most gorgeous men I'd ever seen.

The three of us became inseparable. Our parents were oblivious, and soon lines became blurred, feelings began to grow, and someone's heart was going to get broken. I hoped it wasn't mine.

TABLE OF CONTENTS

PROLOGUE

Cara

I woke up on a Tuesday. My eyes fluttered open, and I glanced around the stark white room. I was surrounded by paper swans that hung from the ceiling, and I held my breath, afraid that I didn't survive my attack. *Was this heaven? Had they somehow let me slip through?* The beeping of machines filled my ears, but a blurred vision of Ellie was what I struggled to focus on.

"I'm here," she spoke, and the beeping of my heart monitor increased as her fingers wrapped around mine.

I tried to speak, but my throat was raw and sore. A nurse was quickly by my side to give me a sip of water.

"Your throat was injured in the attack. Just take it easy," the nurse said as she placed her hand on my shoulder. I kept my eyes locked on El as if she was an illusion that would vanish if I looked away. *Please don't disappear.*

The nurse made a few notes on a clipboard and asked me a few questions before finally giving me a moment alone with Ellie. She leaned down, placing her forehead against mine, and I finally let my eyes close.

"We don't have much time," she whispered as she pulled back to look me in the eye. "You have to tell them that this was a hate crime, Cara."

I shook my head as I croaked out the word no.

"You can't let him get away with this, Cara. I won't let you let him get away with this."

I shook my head again as she held up my cup of water so I could take another drink. "No one can know, El. Please. My mother…"

"Isn't a mother at all if she doesn't care about your safety or happiness."

"What happiness?" I asked, and she gave me a sad smile as her hand covered mine. My knuckles hurt, but I squeezed her back, needing to be closer to her.

"El, there aren't any laws in Georgia to prevent hate crimes."

I watched her lip quiver as that reality hit her. Our own government didn't accept us as equals.

CHAPTER ONE
Ellie

I looked around my new bedroom, my heart heavy in my chest as a tear slipped down my cheek, burning another scar into my soul. *Just a few more hours, and then you can cry into your new pillow.*

"Ellie, time for dinner," my father called from downstairs, his voice an echo from the past. It felt weird to even think of him as my dad. I didn't even remember him outside of the home videos I'd watched obsessively as a child. He'd left my mother without looking back when I was only three years old.

"I'll be right down." I grabbed my mother's necklace that hung against my chest and slid the clasp to the back of my neck, my fingers ghosting over the single round pearl.

Pushing from my bed, I opened my bedroom door and hurried down to the dining room. I offered my father a weak smile as I pulled out a seat across from him and his girlfriend, Dawn. She smiled at me sadly and cleared her throat.

"You have beautiful hair, Ellie. I've always envied girls with thick, dark hair." Dawn tucked her short light-brown hair behind her ear as she scrunched up her nose.

My eyes went to my father's auburn hair as I cut off a bite of my chicken. "I have my mother's hair."

"It's very lovely," she replied, but her voice wavered, making me feel guilty for not being more polite. Even mourning my own mother, I knew bringing her up would make things uncomfortable, and heaven forbid I express my true emotions.

"Thank you, Dawn. That was very kind of you to say." I was raised to respect others. My mother was a stickler for manners and felt kindness was the greatest gift you could give to the world.

"Cara has hair like yours." My father had told me all about Cara on the hour-long drive this morning to his home. She was incredibly kind but had a tough past and was still struggling to move on. He seemed agitated while talking about her, and it made me curious.

As soon as the words left his mouth, the front door opened, and a beautiful brunette entered, sucking all of the air out of the room with her. She was a few months older than me, but her curves were more pronounced, and she was a little taller with deep-green eyes. *Breathtaking.*

"Sorry I'm late!" She hurried in, her smile large and bright. She kissed Dawn on the cheek and then my father, who seemed to tense, causing my stomach to sink. How was this girl so close with my own father, and I was the stranger in their home? Her gaze drifted to me, and I realized I had my eyes narrowed.

"Cara, this is Ellie," my father informed her, and her perfect smile widened.

"Cara McCarthy. It's so great to finally meet you!" She rounded the table, and before I could say a word, her arms were wrapped around my neck as she pulled me against her. I could feel every curve of her body, and I wanted to swallow myself whole for how inadequate I felt next to her. I also wasn't much of a touchy-feely person, and Cara made it apparent that she was.

"Elise Lancaster. Nice to meet you," I mumbled into her hair, which smelled of lilacs and honey and a warm summer breeze. It was amazing birds and tiny woodland creatures didn't follow her around. She didn't seem to be struggling with anything at all, or maybe she was as good as I was at hiding who she really was. I hated that even in my own subconscious I was being mean. I wasn't normally so negative, but after my life had been turned upside down, I was no longer sure I could continue to hide behind this facade. Everything wasn't all right, and I wanted desperately to scream it to the world, but these people were strangers.

As she pulled back to look over my face, her brow furrowed slightly as if she could see I was on the verge on crumbling. I averted my gaze, not wanting her to look me in the eye and see below the surface. *Hold it together. Not much longer.*

"I can't wait to get to know you."

I smiled back, genuinely relieved that at least she was kind; perhaps I would have someone to confide in. Cara slid into the seat next to me, cut into her chicken, and stuck a bite in her mouth. I took another bite as I glanced up at my father, who looked pleased at our interaction, oblivious to my inner turmoil.

"Cara has been volunteering over at Mayweather Hospital for summer break," my father said as he dished more green beans onto his plate, explaining her late arrival.

"Interesting." I took a sip from my glass of water. All I could picture was my mother, lying in a hospital bed with tubes running across her body. I'd never felt so helpless. For all of my planning in life, I wasn't prepared for what had happened, and just the mention of stepping foot into a hospital put my nerves on edge.

"I know they are always looking for extra hands. I could ask around if you're interested." Cara looked at me, her emerald eyes wide as she waited for my response.

"That's kind of you to offer, but I'm not sure I'm up for something like that just yet. Maybe after I'm settled." *I hope I'm long gone before I'm forced to get to know anyone here.*

After a pause in conversation Dawn spoke up, trying to fill the void. "I found this recipe online."

Cara beamed. "It's fantastic."

"It really is wonderful." I smiled, feeling more at ease. I don't know what I expected coming into this new home, but at least their lives seemed to be structured.

"I could teach you how to make it. I'm always happy to have some help in the kitchen."

"Don't let her fool you." Cara elbowed me lightly in the arm. "She will make you peel potatoes for hours," she added with a wink. Everyone chuckled.

"That was one time, and you left half the peel on each one!"

We didn't speak much for the rest of the meal. Although I was curious about my new family, my mind was still trying to absorb the events of this last week.

I volunteered to do the dishes because I felt like an intruder, and to my surprise, Cara offered to help me. I scrubbed the plates, and she rinsed them and stuck them in the rack to dry, humming a song I couldn't place.

"I'm really glad you're here, Ellie." She slipped her hand down into the soapy water and wrapped her fingers around mine, giving them a gentle squeeze. "I'm really sorry to hear about your mother. It's not so bad here, I promise. You will make friends in no time."

"Thank you…for being so nice."

She released my hand and went back to humming her song. I sighed, not realizing I'd been holding my breath. *Why did her touch feel so…personal?*

"Is there a library close by?"

"There is one right by the high school, down on Jefferson Street. What type of book are you looking for?" Dawn's voice startled me. I'd forgotten she was still in the room.

"Just something to get lost in." I shrugged, avoiding her eyes as Dawn brought our glasses over from the table and set them on the counter.

"Cara has an e-reader. I'm sure she wouldn't mind letting you look at it."

"Yeah, you can borrow it anytime you like. It's mostly sad stuff, but I'm sure there is something on there you'll like," she added with a wink when Dawn wasn't looking, and I couldn't help but smile.

"Thanks."

We finished up our work before I slipped up to my new bedroom and lay on the twin-size bed, my eyes unfocused on the blank walls. After about an hour there was a light tapping at my door. My father peeked his head through as he glanced at the still-packed boxes stacked along the wall.

"Dawn and I are going to bed. I have an early day tomorrow. If you need anything, don't hesitate to ask." His eyes were trained on me for a moment before he added what felt like an afterthought. "It's great to have you here, Ellie. I think it will be really good for you and Cara."

I nodded, but another stabbing pain ached through my chest. I needed a father fifteen years ago; now all I wanted was my mom. He pulled my door closed, and I listened to his footsteps retreat down the hallway.

I decided that even though I didn't plan to live here very long, I still needed to unpack a few of my things. Reluctantly, I got up from my bed and flipped open a box. Inside were pictures of my mother and me together. The tears slipped easily from my eyes as I looked at her smiling, carefree face. I set them on my dresser and pulled out my notebooks that were full of life goals and plans for my future. My sadness turned to anger as I thought of all of the plans my mother had that would be left undone. We spent our days making sure we would have a better tomorrow, and now that had been ripped from our lives.

For the first time, I questioned it all. As my vision blurred I ground my teeth together, ripping out page after page of my ideal future, letting it fall to the ground around me. Sobs ripped from my chest as I fell to my knees. I'd shed a few tears since my mother's death, but this was the first moment I'd finally been able to let the walls come down. No one was around to see me crumble, and it was liberating to break apart without judgment.

There was a quiet tapping, and I stifled my cries enough to realize someone was at my door.

"Ellie?" Cara called out. I quickly wiped the tears from my cheeks and cleared my throat. *No, not now. You can't see me like this.*

"Yes?"

"Can I come in?"

I looked around at the cluttered mess of papers, the chaos in the otherwise orderly room. It was a direct reflection of the turmoil that was plaguing me. I began gathering up the scraps of crumpled paper in a desperate attempt to hide my breakdown.

"I'm getting ready for bed," I called out as I feverishly struggled to collect the evidence. The click of the door unlatching caused my head to shoot up, and I locked eyes with Cara. I must have looked like an absolute mess, and I could see the pity in her eyes.

"I was just..." A few stray papers fell from my arms and fluttered to the hardwood floor. A shudder shook my chest as I dropped the remnants of my abandoned future, clasping my hand over my mouth. Cara rushed to my side, dropping to her knees and wrapping her arms around me. I fell apart, crying into her hair, clinging desperately to the kindness of this stranger. I had no one else. Her hand slowly stroked the back of my head as she began humming the same haunting tune that she had while we were washing dishes together.

"It's going to be okay," she whispered before humming again. All I could do was shake my head, refusing to believe life could ever be the same again. "It gets easier."

My fingers gripped the back of her shirt, desperate to not feel so alone. After what felt like an eternity I whispered, "It's never going to be the same."

She pulled me back from her embrace, her thumbs running over my dampened cheeks as my eyes fluttered closed momentarily. "It doesn't need to be the same, but it *will* get better. I promise." Her eyes were locked on mine, her expression serious. I swallowed back my self-pity and nodded, because something in her eyes told me she was speaking from experience. She gave me a small smile before tucking my hair behind my ears. "I brought you my e-reader. I thought you might want something to occupy your mind."

I glanced to the floor beside us at the small square device. "Thank you. You didn't need to do that."

"If you want to talk about it..."

I pushed to my feet, sniffling. "No. I'm fine. I just lost it for a minute, but I'm okay. Really." I forced a smile through the crippling agony.

Her eyes scanned me as she grabbed the device and stood as well. "It's okay to not be fine, Ellie. I understand." *You couldn't possibly.*

"I don't think anyone else could understand." I took the e-reader from her hand and nodded once. She didn't say anything else; as she turned and left the room, I looked down at the mess of papers around me. My world was a disorganized upheaval.

I tossed the device on my new bed as I exhaled deeply, groaning with regret for how I'd treated the one person who'd shown me kindness.

I slipped down the hall to the bathroom to splash some cold water on my face. As my eyes met my reflection, I winced at the puffy, pink-stained face staring back at me, the happiness no longer evident in my soil-colored eyes.

I brushed my teeth and headed back toward my room. Cara's room was just above the staircase. The light was off but I could see a flicker of light from a television. I tiptoed down the hall and lightly tapped on the door, needing to let her know that I wasn't the mess she'd witnessed. There was no response, so I knocked again before turning the knob and slowly pushing it open. The room was empty as I slipped inside, my eyes dancing over the flickering space. Her bedspread was vibrant red, a direct contrast to the earthy tones of mine. I pulled the door closed again, and I slipped back into my own room and curled up in a ball in the center of my bed. I clicked the button on the bottom of the electronic library and flicked my finger across the screen to try to decide which cover looked most appealing. Nothing caught my attention and I was going to forgo the idea all together until the title *The Good Girls* caught my attention. The book had been favorited by Cara, and it made me curious. The cover was a teenage girl in a beautiful dress, but there was a haunting sadness in her eyes. That's exactly how I felt: haunted. I swiped my finger over the cover and began to read, page by page, until the words were too blurred to comprehend.

Images of the heroine named Claire, struggling through her life to be the person everyone expected of her, plagued my dreams. She lived vicariously through elaborate fantasies.

I tossed and turned as I imagined cutting loose from everything I'd been told was right and finally began living my life and enjoying it. But even in my dreams I couldn't imagine being able to be happy again, now that I'd lost my mother. My imagination was broken, like my heart.

CHAPTER TWO
Cara

My heart began to beat again on a Tuesday. Watching Ellie fall apart at the loss of her mother caused crippling pain to radiate through my chest. I pulled the picture of my mom from my top dresser drawer and ran my fingertips over her smiling face. *You're a bigger liar than I am.* It had been months since I'd laid eyes on her, and it wasn't because she'd passed away, it was because she chose to leave my life.

I wiped a stray tear from my cheek and shoved the picture back in its hiding spot before grabbing my phone and falling across my bed on my stomach. I typed a quick text to Tristan in hopes he could get me out of the house for a few hours. He responded after a minute that he would be by to pick me up in twenty minutes.

I tossed my phone on my pillow and freshened up my makeup, dabbing concealer under my eyes to hide the puffy redness, the truth of how I really felt inside. I felt guilty for leaving Ellie alone, but I didn't know how I could help her deal with the pain when I still was unable to deal with my own. If I was honest, I had hugged her just to get a reaction from David. After he'd warned me to stay away from his daughter, it made me feel dirty, unwanted. I needed to show him that it was possible for someone to care about me. Who better than his precious Ellie? But one look into her sad eyes made me sick that I'd ever considered using her. I'd been like her when I showed up here, and I would have given anything for someone to show me some compassion. *I won't let Ellie suffer like I did.*

We were worlds apart, adjoined by a thin wall that allowed me to hear her quiet sobs. Even though David had taken me in, I was baggage dragged along by Dawn. His caring for me was a consolation prize for him to be able to take the next step with his girlfriend.

Dawn was a truly caring soul, so her disapproval of who I was as a person didn't cause her to flinch when I needed a helping hand. "Love the sinner but hate the sin," she used to say, as if that somehow would make me feel better. It didn't. It only made me feel dirty and unwanted. I was a bad seed but a good deed, another check mark on her ticket to heaven. I snorted to myself—as if God judged you based on a point system, and I was failing simply by not understanding the questions he was asking of us. What does he want from me? I'm only human, created in his image and trying to live up to the standards of a God. His disappointment in me is his own failure, not mine. My free will is not freedom at all. I have to be a certain person, follow arbitrary rules set by his own creations, or be locked away in a cage like a circus animal, poked and prodded by society until I give in and become one of them.

But that was a different lifetime for me. I no longer believed in the childhood fairy tales of heaven and hell, good and evil. The lines were a blur of blood and tears. Now I was the girl who harbored secrets and regrets while smiling. I wished I could be more like Ellie, but I hated myself too much to ever have so much self-respect.

Changing into a short jean skirt and wedge sandals, I looked myself over in the full-length mirror that hung on the back of my door. *Good enough.*

I snuck out of my room and carefully made my way to the darkened downstairs, feeling as if it was some metaphor of me slipping closer to hell. The house was eerily quiet, the world dreaming of a better tomorrow as I struggled to escape.

I made my way down the driveway, only illuminated by the dim lighting of a street lamp from the main road. Sinking down on the curb, I waited for my boyfriend to arrive.

He pulled up moments later with a bright grin on his handsome face, rubbing his fingers over the few days' worth of stubble along his jaw. His blue eyes sparkled in the dim overhead lighting that popped on when I pulled open the passenger-side door. I slid across the seat and pulled the door closed, cloaking us in darkness.

"Everything all right?" he asked as we drove away. *Nothing is all right. It never has been.*

"Perfect," I purred as I began to undo the button to his jeans. He adjusted in his seat so I could lower his zipper. *I don't want to think; I just want to forget.*

"Yes, you are," he said with a deep laugh as I felt the car swerve when I wrapped my fingers around his length, slowly stroking the smooth skin. I glanced up at his clenched jaw, the muscles ticking underneath his skin as he stared at the road ahead, struggling to concentrate. His long fingers slid into my hair, encouraging me to take it a step further. I smiled as I slid my tongue over his tip, coating my taste buds with his salty flavor. It was hard not to cringe.

"Fuck," he groaned. His grip on my hair tightened, and I took him deep into my throat. He pulled off to the side of the road into the darkness and put the car in park, killing the headlights. Slow classic rock played in the background, muffling his quiet moans as I continued to tease him with my tongue.

"Jesus, what's gotten into you tonight?"

I glanced up at him and continued to stroke with my hand. "I was hoping you," I replied coyly.

He nodded his head. "Then get over here."

I sat up, tucking my hair behind my ear before sliding one of my legs over him, hiking my skirt up around my waist.

Sliding my panties to the side, I rubbed his head against my entrance.

"Baby, fuck," he groaned, his fingers gripping my hips. "I need to put on a condom."

"I'm on the pill. I want to feel you." I panted as I lowered myself slowly onto him. His eyes fell closed. I closed mine as well, getting lost in the sensation and letting my mind empty all of today's worries. My hips rose and fell, torturously slow as my mouth hovered over Tristan's, inhaling his minty air.

"You are so fucking sexy." Tristan's hands pulled down on my hips, causing me to whimper as he impaled me on his thickness before his fingers slid under my shirt and over my breast. Tristan was the first boy I'd ever slept with. We'd only been dating a couple of months, but I was desperate to move on with my life as soon as possible and forget my ex.

His hands roamed over my skin as if he couldn't get close enough to me. I looped my arms around his neck as his teeth tugged at my earlobe. I felt him grow harder and moved faster, helping him find his release, his body jerking below me with a guttural groan.

As he released into me, my body began to tighten around him, shuddering as I came undone in his arms, my brief escape from reality over.

He kissed my cheek and nose before his lips were on mine.

"That was amazing." He pulled back to look me in the eye as he tucked my hair behind my ears.

I slid off his lap, adjusted my clothing, and pulled my skirt back over my hips.

"Where do you want to go?" I asked, hoping he wanted to hang out for a while before I'd have to go back home. *I don't ever want to go back.*

"Something going on at home?" he asked as we pulled back out onto the street.

Shrugging, I chewed on my thumb as I stared out of the passenger window, the houses blurring by. "David's daughter came to stay with us."

"You don't like her?"

I shrugged again. "She's all right. We're the same age."

"Why didn't you invite her out with us?" *Because you'd take one look at her and realize she is so much better than I am.*

"I just met her, Tristan. What if she goes running back to her daddy and tells him I sneak out with you every night? David already hates me. I couldn't survive in this place if I didn't have you."

Tristan reached over and took my hand in his, pulling it up to his mouth and placing a kiss on the back of it. "Nothing would stop me from seeing you—not even that fucking asshole." His gaze was cold, almost frightening.

I nodded, but I knew that wasn't true. I'd been abandoned before, and one of those people happened to be my own mother. I smiled weakly back at him, trying my best to convince him that I believed his words. *You'll get tired of me or find someone else.*

"Can we just drive around for a little while? I really don't feel like partying."

"Whatever you want, babe."

For the next two hours, I sang along to songs from the nineties as we made our way down nearly every street in town and got high. I let the world evaporate around me as I heard a small giggle in the back of my mind. It was the same sound that haunted my dreams, and I struggled to suppress the memories and enjoy the high, but it became overbearing.

I traced Tristan's bicep with the pad of my finger, laughing when he looked over at me, shaking his head.

"What?" he asked as he turned down another dark road.

"I dunno." I pulled my feet up onto the dashboard, dragging my hands down my thighs.

"Again?" His eyebrow shot up as he glanced over at my legs. "Babe, I'm tired, and I got to get you back home."

I groaned, jutting my bottom lip out in a pout as we turned around and headed back toward my house.

"You know we can't keep this pace up when we both have classes, right?"

"Then why waste the little bit of time we have now?" I asked as I leaned over and ran my palm against his jeans, his cock hardening under my touch.

"I have stuff to do tomorrow. My mom is coming out to visit."

"Am I going to get to meet her?" I was shocked. This was the first I was hearing that his family would be visiting. Tristan was raised here, but his family moved away when his father got offered a job in Chicago.

"Not tomorrow." He dismissed the idea and turned up the radio. I stared at him for a moment before turning the volume back down.

"Why not?" *Why am I not good enough?*

"Come on, Cara. It's just a bad time."

"Why? Are you not as serious about us as I am?"

"It's not that." He shook his head as he took my hand in his. "My mom is just really conservative. I told you about how I was raised." *Like I was raised, and even my own mother couldn't find it in her heart to love me.*

"And?" I pulled my hand free and crossed my arms over my chest.

"Well, you're just kind of…I dunno…" *Worthless.*

"What?" My voice rose as I stared daggers into the side of his face. "I'm what?" *Say it. Look me in the eye and tell me what you really think of me.*

"She just wouldn't approve of us." He bit this out as he gave me a sympathetic glance, but I could see his knuckles whiten as he gripped the wheel tighter. He was struggling to control his temper, and I was pushing him too far, but I didn't care.

"Oh, really? Would she approve of her son who gets his girlfriend high and fucks her in his car along the road?"

"Are you fucking serious?" He pulled up to the curb just outside of my driveway and turned off the engine, turning to face me.

"What do you care what she thinks?" *It's because this is about what you think of me. Just say it.*

"I don't." He ran his hands roughly through his hair.

"It's you." My voice was barely audible. "You're ashamed of me. You're embarrassed."

I opened my door as he reached over and grabbed my wrist so tightly it felt as if the bones would crumble beneath his fingers.

"Don't walk away from me, Cara."

"It's late. I have to go."

His fingers loosened slightly, and I pulled my hand free as I got out of the car, bending down to look him in the eye. "I'm embarrassed to be dating you right now, too." With that I slammed the door and took off down the road, stumbling on the gravel under my feet.

CHAPTER THREE
Ellie

When I awoke the sun was blinding me, and I stretched, my entire body aching from the sadness of the night before. I glanced to the alarm clock on the stand beside the bed and jumped when I noticed it was nearly eleven. It took me a moment to remember I didn't need to be at the bakery to help Mom, and the dread settled back into my chest. My eyes fell to the electronic reader, and I wanted to disappear into my beige blanket. I was raised to be proper and presentable, and I'd already lost it on my first night. *Cara must think I'm pathetic.*

I pulled open a box labeled CLOTHING and grabbed a nice blue sundress that I had gotten a few months ago, along with my undies. I hurried down the hall to the bathroom and turned on the shower. I usually had to let it run a few minutes for it to get warm at my old home, but here it was nearly instantaneous. *At least there's one bright side to living here*, I thought as I pulled off my clothing and dropped it to the floor.

As I dragged back the floral curtain, my eyes danced over the many different bottles of shampoos and conditioners. I'd always used the ninety-nine-cent kind from the local supermarket. I stepped under the warm spray and began picking up the different bottles, flipping open the lids, and smelling them. I smiled as I recognized the lilac scent of Cara.

I poured the creamy liquid into my hand and massaged it in my hair, the warm water making me feel more awake.

I rushed through my normal shower routine, not wanting to waste the hot water, even if they had it in abundance here. Dressing quickly, I combed my fingers through my damp hair to make sure it wasn't tangled. I glanced over my appearance in the mirror. My eyes were no longer swollen and puffy, and I could pass for presentable. That would have to do.

I made my way downstairs to find Cara flipping through the channels in the family room, wearing jeans and a T-shirt, making me feel overdressed for the day. Her face lit up when she noticed me, and she patted the cushion beside her. I sat down, still embarrassed by her witnessing my breakdown last night. "I…ugh…wanted to thank you for last night."

"What happened last night?" My father was standing in the doorway in a crisp, white button-down shirt and dark-gray slacks. He was fumbling with his cuff link, but his gaze was on us.

"I just lent Ellie my e-reader. She's a book nerd like me," Cara replied, her eyes coming to me before she plastered on her perfect smile. The tension between them was palpable.

"Oh, that's wonderful. What book are you reading?" he asked dryly.

I cleared my throat, surprised Cara had kept my breakdown a secret, but it felt as though she had her own reasons for the omission. "*Pride and Prejudice*. It was Mom's favorite." *You remember the woman you abandoned, don't you?*

He nodded, looking uncomfortable at the mention of my mother. "I'm heading back to the office. I have a late meeting with another accountant, and Dawn is working a double shift, so I won't see you until late. If you need anything just call my cell." *I'd made it this long without you, I think I can manage.*

"Bye," we both called back in unison. We waited to hear the front door click shut before we looked at each other.

"Thank you for not telling him. I don't really know him enough yet to want to talk about my mom to him. It's still too…new."

"If you do want someone to talk about it with, I meant what I said last night."

"I appreciate that. Speaking of last night, I wanted to thank you, but when I went to your room, you weren't there."

"Oh, I just went for a walk to clear my head." She looked down at the remote in her hand. My gaze followed hers as I took in the purpling bruise on her wrist. *How would someone get a bruise like that?*

"Oh," I replied, not certain I believed her. Maybe there was more to Cara than the perfect layer I'd seen, and I wished I'd pushed my father to tell me more about her on the drive here, but my mind was elsewhere.

Her eyes narrowed as she tilted her head slightly. "*Pride and Prejudice*, huh?" The corners of her mouth turned up into a grin.

"It's a classic." I cleared my throat and turned my attention to the television.

"Mm-hmm…" She turned up the volume, and we both relaxed against the back of the couch. Cara clicked on the On Demand on her cable and hit play on a movie called *Closer*. "Speaking of classics." I settled in, smiling when it started off as what looked like your standard love story, but as the movie continued on, I realized it was more about lies and lust than love. Still, I was entranced by the characters and their desperate need to feel wanted.

No one was who they said they were and while I could never imagine my life as a stripper, I could relate to the feeling of never revealing who you truly are.

"What did you think?" Cara turned to me.

I scrunched up my nose. "It was…interesting." *And incredibly awkward to watch a girl strip on screen next to someone I barely know.*

"Interesting," she repeated. "I think it's sad. There is no point to love if it doesn't last forever."

Her words struck me. I hadn't expected such a deep statement coming from her. As the credits rolled on the screen Cara stood and set the remote on the coffee table.

"You want to get some lunch? I'd love to see a little bit of the town," I suggested as I stood up. *I need out of this place before I go insane.*

Cara eyed me for a moment and shook her head. "I have some stuff I need to do, but maybe some other time."

"Oh...okay," I replied as she gave me a quick smile before leaving the room. I'd thought maybe I'd finally made a friend, but it occurred to me that I had just lost my mother; she was being nice to me, as anyone would in her situation.

Not wanting to figure out my way on my own and not feeling comfortable enough to rummage through their kitchen, I headed back to my room instead.

I cleaned up the paper mess on my floor, tossing all of the scraps back into the box the notebook had come from before deciding to read a few chapters. With the e-reader in my hand, I hit the main menu and clicked on the search bar. Typing in *Pride and Prejudice*, I waited for the cover to pop up, but instead I got a message that the book was not on this device. *Shit.*

Cara knew I was lying to her, but she didn't call me out on it. I pulled back up the book I had been reading and let myself get lost in the story, desperate to escape reality if even for a few hours.

The heroine, Claire, was now daydreaming she was at a bar with a fake ID as she flirted unabashedly with a handsome stranger a few stools down from her, not even batting an eye that he was already there with another woman. Within minutes she had him begging for the opportunity to take her back to his place so he could watch her with his girlfriend. I'd read a lot of romance novels, but most glossed over the sexual encounters. This book gave step-by-step detail for every move that they had made, from the man stroking himself to Claire having her legs splayed as the girlfriend's head dipped between them.

I locked the screen and tossed the device beside me on the bed. This was not the kind of book I'd pictured Cara reading, and it made me even more curious about her. There was something hidden behind her smirk, a secret that I just couldn't read, and I wanted to know what it was.

My stomach was panging with hunger from missing the first two meals of the day, but with no other options, I headed to the bathroom and filled up a glass with water.

I gulped it down and refilled it, taking smaller sips this time, when I heard Cara's muffled voice coming from her room. She sounded angry, but she was trying to keep herself quiet. Dawn and David were both at work, so I knew it was me she was trying to keep quiet for.

With my glass of water in hand, I quietly made my way toward my bedroom, pausing at the entrance as I strained to listen to her words.

"No. You know that's wrong!" There was a pause, and I realized she must have been on a phone. "Fine. Whatever!"

Just then her bedroom door opened, and I was so startled the glass of water slipped from my hand, shattering as it hit the wooden floor. *Shit. Busted.*

"What are you doing out here?" she snapped. Cara looked angry and caught off-guard as I took a step forward, searing pain traveling from my heel and up my calf. I cried out in shock as she rushed over to me, grabbing my sides and helping to guide me into my room. I sat down on the edge of my bed as she lifted my foot in her hand, examining the damage.

"How is it?" *Do you hate me yet?*

She looked at me, her eyebrows pulled together before she looked back at my foot, clearly not pleased with finding me in the hall. "It's just a little piece of glass. Wait here, I'll grab the tweezers and a Band-Aid." She went to the bathroom and retrieved the supplies along with a brown bottle of peroxide.

"Everything okay?" I asked, and she just shook her head in frustration as she pulled the glass from my foot. "Ouch!" This was a side to Cara that I hadn't seen, another layer unraveling the mystery. Her fingers slid soothingly against the base of my foot.

"Everything is fine. Why do you ask?" Her tone was sharp, but she was gentle as she worked on my injury.

"I just heard you, and you sounded upset."

"When you were eavesdropping?" Her gaze flicked to mine, eyebrow arched. She dumped peroxide onto a cotton ball and rubbed it over my cut.

"I wasn't...I was getting a drink from the bathroom; hence, the broken glass."

"You're not a good liar. But I did hear you crying last night, and that's why I came to bring you the e-reader. So I guess we're even." She sighed loudly as she put the

Band-Aid in place and stood. "Everything is fine. I just had a disagreement with someone…a friend."

"At least you have friends," I mumbled, and Cara's expression softened.

"I think you're going to live, but you may just want to drink the bottled water in the fridge from now on. It's less dangerous." Her tone was less hostile and more sarcastic. I relaxed, thankful she didn't hate me already.

"I didn't want to just take anything without asking. I didn't know you were even here until I heard you talking."

"You live here, Ellie. If you seriously wait for permission for every little thing in life, you will never be happy. If you want something, take it."

She turned to leave the room, hopping over the mess I'd made. "I'll grab the broom and dustpan from the laundry room."

Cara returned a few minutes later with the broom. I slipped on my sandals and walked to my door.

"I can get that. It's my mess." I reached for the dustpan, but she pulled her arm back.

"It's not a big deal. Besides, you'd probably just cut yourself again," she said with a small laugh. "Where did you go for lunch?" She looked up when I didn't respond. "You wouldn't even take a water from the fridge. If you didn't go out, what have you eaten all day?"

"I'm fine. I wasn't really that hungry anyway." I shook my head but my stomach panged again at just the mention of food. Cara finished sliding the glass onto the pan and stood.

"Come on. I'll make us something. Dawn and David won't be home until late, and I don't want to get blamed for letting you wither away."

"Thank you." I followed her down to the kitchen, settling into one of the chairs at the table as she searched the fridge for something to eat.

She sat a head of lettuce on the table along with a box of cherry tomatoes and other salad supplies. "What dressing do you like?" she called over her shoulder.

"French."

She turned to look at me, eyes narrowed. I held her gaze, my face impassive.

She shook her head slowly as she tried to suppress a smile. "You're lying again."

"How can you tell?"

She shrugged as she continued to get more supplies from the fridge. "It's a gift…and a curse. You show your emotions on your face, dummy. It's not that hard to tell." She glanced back to me. "So what do you *really* want?"

"Ranch, if you have it."

She stood up smiling, shaking the bottle. "I eat it on nearly everything." Kicking the fridge closed with her foot, she grabbed us each a bowl from the cupboard and began to make our salads.

"What are the schools like here?" I asked, feeling like a child for not preparing my own food.

Cara shrugged as she popped a tiny tomato in her mouth. "It's high school. Pure hell." she wrinkled her nose. "I was only here for a few months of this last year, so it wasn't that great, but this year I'll be a senior, so it should be fun."

I almost asked her if she had lived with her father before ending up here, but I knew I'd be expected to talk about my mom, and I wasn't ready for that yet. "At least I'll know you. I hope we have a few classes together." I grabbed one of the tomatoes and popped it in my mouth.

"You're seventeen, right?"

"Until March," I replied with a groan. I reached for a mushroom, and Cara smacked my hand lightly. We both laughed.

"I'll be eighteen in a few weeks. I can't wait. I want to get out of this place as soon as possible."

My stomach sank at the thought of losing the only person I'd know at school. Dawn and David didn't seem very hands-on, but they also didn't seem like people to run *from*, which made me wonder if there was someone she was running *toward*. I realized I was probably making a face and quickly tried to make my expression neutral.

"But obviously, that would take money, and I have none," she added, making me feel more at ease.

Cara slid the bowl over to me and grabbed us each a fork from the drawer. She took a seat across from me, and we both began to eat. I moaned as I took a large bite.

"I know my salads are good, but seriously?"

I felt my cheeks heat in embarrassment. "I haven't eaten since last night. I think cardboard would taste delicious right now."

"Ouch. I liked it better when you were moaning." She laughed and shook her head before clearing her throat. "So what book are you *really* reading?" Her eyebrow rose as she called me out on my lie.

"Where'd you *really* go last night?" *Something tells me you're more fascinating than the book I've been reading.*

Her eyes narrowed as she fought against a smirk, and for a second it felt like she knew what I was thinking. "I'm not ready to divulge all of my secrets just yet."

"Fair enough." I let it go, but now I was really curious about her.

We finished our salads, and Cara took our bowls. "It's best if I get this. I don't want to have to clean any more wounds."

"You're not going to let that go, are you?" I asked as I grabbed us each a bottle of water from the fridge.

"Not until I get some better dirt on you," she teased as she rinsed out plates and took the drink with a thanks. "I'm going to go run through the shower."

"Yeah, I should probably unpack a few boxes," I said as I followed her up the stairs. I thanked her again for the food, slipped inside my room, and lay on my stomach across my bed. I was dying to get back into the book I was reading, and the last thing I wanted was to be reminded of my life prior to living here. It was too painful.

Cara appeared in my doorway and dropped a towel on my water mess. "Wouldn't want you to slip," she joked as she headed back down the hall.

When I heard the bathroom door close I unlocked the screen, chewing my lower lip as I devoured a few more chapters of my book, getting lost in the illicit debauchery. After a long night in the stranger's apartment that earned her nice pay, the heroine was now startled back into reality, sitting in one of her college classes and listening to her professor's lecture. I began to skim the pages, wanting to know what her next secret encounter would be. The dull repetition of her everyday life was like looking into a mirror, and I wanted it to fog over, allowing me to drift off in my own subconscious.

"Skipping to the good parts?" I jumped, turning on my side to see a smirking Cara with a towel held against her chest. It wasn't wrapped around her and I could see her bare tan hips on either side of the white fabric that stopped just low enough not to reveal her private parts. *Holy shit. I wished I was as comfortable with myself as she seems to be. Life must be effortless when you look like absolute perfection.*

She bent down closer to me, and I held my breath, uncertain of what she was going to do. Embarrassment washed over me as she picked up the e-reader. I grabbed it, but she gripped it tightly as she began to read aloud. "His hand slid into my panties, and I gasped as he entered me with two of his long fingers." She finally released her grip and let me take the e-reader back as I lay frozen in horror.

"I didn't think you'd be into that kind of stuff, Ellie. You're full of surprises." She shook her head in mock disapproval as she straightened. "And here I thought you were one of the *good girls.*"

"You're one to talk. It's your book," I retorted.

She laughed, shaking her head and causing her long damp hair to cling to her sun-kissed skin. "I'm sorry. It's just so easy to cause you to blush. It's cute." She grabbed the edges of her towel and pulled them around her to cover her backside as well before heading to her own room.

I groaned, flopping onto my back as I wallowed in humiliation. I'll return it to Cara and find the local library tomorrow. But first, I at least needed to know how it ended. I read as fast as I could, chapter after chapter until the sun sank outside of my window. My father and Dawn came home from work. They were both exhausted and turned in without even saying a word.

CHAPTER FOUR

Cara

Dropping the towel just inside my door, I grabbed my makeup bag from my dresser, sat down on the edge of my bed, and began to paint the pretty illusion of contentment on my face.

My mind drifted to the look on Ellie's face as I busted her reading that book. *Was she checking me out, or had I imagined it?* Her innocence made me yearn for the days when I never saw myself as wrong or bad. It made me envious of her, but at the same time I was curious about how she could hold herself together, so sure of herself. I wanted to learn from her.

It was in this moment I decided I wasn't going to avoid Ellie any longer. I was going to get to know her, bring her out of her shell. Right now I felt like I needed someone on my side as well, and it might do us both some good.

Once I finished my makeup, I blow-dried my hair and straightened it before looking myself over in the mirror. I was pretty certain Ellie's eyes had lingered on my exposed flesh. I ran my hand over my stomach, turning sideways to examine myself. I hated that even my own boyfriend felt like I was something to be hidden away in a closet.

Huffing, I went to my dresser and pulled out a pair of turquoise lace panties and slid them up over my hips. Grabbing my favorite vintage Monkeys tank top and a pair of fitted jeans, I finished dressing before falling back on my bed and staring at the ceiling. Normally, I'd fill the void between now and sneaking out with reading, but Ellie had my e-reader. *I wonder what sordid chapter she's reading now.*

I flipped my cell over in my hand, wanting to text Tristan but forcing myself to wait until he apologized first. He was probably out with his mother right now. After the call I'd had earlier today, I really wanted to make things right between us.

I sent him a quick text telling him that I didn't want to fight before pulling open my laptop and clicking on my browser reading application.

I smiled when it asked me to sync to the last page read in *The Good Girls*. Chewing on my lip, I clicked yes as my eyes scanned the new location. I was shocked that she hadn't quit reading it. There was a dirty side to her, and it made me want to get to know her more.

Ellie was reading chapter 14, and I knew exactly which part she was on. It was a scene where the main character, Claire, was fantasizing about sleeping with her best friend and not just any friend, but another female.

My eyes scanned over the digital pages line after line as the story played out in my head.

My body was running hot as I pictured the girls grinding together on the dance floor as the world around them fell away. I decided to relieve some stress of my own, and I stood from the computer and fell back on my bed. Unzipping my jeans, I let my eyes flutter closed as my fingers dipped below the edge of my panties and disappeared beneath the lacy fabric.

I pressed against my damp clit as my hips rolled forward to create more friction against my smooth flesh. I let the story continue to roll through my mind and wondered if Ellie was doing the same. My eyes flew open in horror, but my fingers continued to move against me. I squeezed my eyes shut again, picturing Tristan's tanned, stubbled face between my thighs as his tongue lapped against me with expert precision. Quiet pants escaped my lips as I pressed my head back against my pillow.

My release was fast and hard, and I was certain someone had to have heard the quiet moans that resonated from the back of my throat. As soon as the pulsing ebbed, I was immediately awash with shame. *What the hell was I doing?* I buttoned my pants and hurried to the bathroom, where I took a scalding shower, scrubbing my skin so hard I thought it would leave a road rash.

My mind was a flurry of memories and pain, not because I'd fantasized about Ellie, but because for the first time, I wasn't thinking about Tatum. My heart broke as I pictured her strawberry-blond curls splayed across my pillow as we laughed and told each other secrets until the sun came up.

We'd been best friends for years, absolutely inseparable. She'd always join my family at church on Sundays, and I would go camping with her and her father every May. We were often teased by the boys at school about how close we were. Tatum would flip out and yell at them and tell them we were like sisters. I would just smile and know that they wished they'd gotten to spend so much time with her.

I dragged the razor over my calf as my eyes blurred, mixing my tears with conditioner. I could still see the horror on her face, though, when she and I were kissing, claiming it was practice for the day we met a guy we really liked. We'd done it countless times and our make-out sessions had gotten hot and heavy on many occasions, but this day was different. We'd become too comfortable in who we were and forgot how the world around us would judge us if they ever found out. We learned our lesson the hard way when Tatum's father caught us together in her living room when he was supposed to be working late.

A man I looked up to and treated me as if I were one of his own now looked at me in disgust, as if I'd just murdered someone. And in his eyes, I had. I'd killed the perfect image of his precious baby girl. But instead of standing up for what we had, Tatum was afraid, and she denied our love for each other, telling him that I had kissed her out of nowhere.

After a humiliating phone call with my mother and then being forced to talk to the priest at our church, I was deemed unworthy of compassion or love and sent to live with my mother's friend Dawn, the only person left who could look me in the eye. But living with Dawn came with a price, and that was having to live with David.

"Shit." A sob ripped from my chest as the blur became crimson running down my leg. I rinsed my hair quickly before holding my leg under the water, letting the redness swirl down the drain.

I needed to forget about Tatum and move on with my life. I *had* moved on with my life. Tristan was a good guy who had goals and treated me well. I'd never had someone stand up for me and protect me the way he did. I only wished I could trust him with my secrets, but I was too afraid he'd judge me like my mother, and I'd lose him, too.

I stepped out of the shower onto the fluffy white bath mat, a drop of crimson slithered down my leg and spread out onto the white tuffs of fabric. Grabbing the soap, I wet a washcloth and scrubbed the spot until it was a faded pink.

Next, I tended to my own injury as I did earlier with Ellie, cleaning and bandaging the tiny nick. I slipped a towel around my waist and quietly crept back to my room.

I let the towel pool on the floor around my feet and made my way to my dresser. I grabbed a pair of jeans and a yellow tank top with matching yellow panties and pulled them on quickly. I reapplied my makeup and straightened my hair, feeling lethargic after a good cry but still wanting to escape this place for a little while. I finished off my look with assorted bangle bracelets that hid the ugly bruises on my wrists behind something shiny and beautiful.

I grabbed my phone, and to my surprise Tristan had texted me back while I had been in the shower. He apologized for upsetting me last night and told me that he wasn't ashamed of me at all, but he didn't want to subject me to his judgmental parents, whom he avoided at all costs.

My thoughts drifted to Ellie and the strain between her and David. I had to get her out of here, even for a little bit, because I owed her. She had helped me escape the memory of Tatum, even if momentarily, and even though she wasn't aware of it.

CHAPTER FIVE
Ellie

I wasn't the least bit tired, but there was nothing else to do. I rose from my bed and flipped open one of the boxes, searching through my clothing for something to sleep in as my door squeaked open behind me. I turned, startled as Cara laughed, clicking the door closed behind her. Her hair was straightened, her emerald eyes lined in black.

"What are you doing?" she asked.

I held up a pair of sweat pants. "Getting ready for bed. What are *you* doing?"

Her eyebrows pulled together as she shook her head. "No you're not. We're going out."

"Oh, I don't think my father would like that."

Cara rolled her eyes as she pushed from the door and walked toward me, flopping down on my bed. "What would *you* like, Ellie? No offense, but I know him, and he is oblivious to everything…like the fact that technically what I do at the hospital is community service, and it ended weeks ago. Or the fact that his daughter is in desperate need of his attention."

"None taken," I huffed as I stood, and my eyes drifted down Cara's torso to her fingers that were playing with a small silver ring looped in her belly button.

"It's cute, right?"

My eyes snapped back to her smiling face. "If you like that sort of stuff."

She laughed as she pulled her pale yellow shirt down to cover her stomach. "Oh, come on, Ellie. Dawn and David aren't here. You can drop the act. I already caught you reading porn."

"What act? And do you really call your mother by her first name?" I completely ignored her porn comment, because I knew she was just trying to get a rise out of me.

"This perfect little good-girl act, and she's *not* my mother." She stood from the bed and snatched the sweat pants from my hand. "I can tell when you're lying."

"It's not an act," I snapped. I reached for my pants, and she held them behind her back. I wanted to press her about Dawn not being her mother, but asking would be rude, and regardless of how Cara was acting now, I would keep my composure. I didn't like how easily Cara was able to make me squirm.

"Yes it is." Her head cocked to the side as she looked me over, clearly amused. "Just come out for a little while. I want to get to know you, and I promise you won't get in any trouble." She drug her finger over her heart in a cross motion. "You wanted to know where I go when I sneak out. Here's your chance. I figured I owed you after picking on you, and maybe deep down under that prim and proper dress"—she paused as her eyes looked me over—"*maybe* there is a wild side to you."

As uncertain as I was about Cara, I really did need to get out of this house before I lost my mind. Two days, and I was already wanting to claw at the walls. This was my chance to step outside of the structured world I'd built for myself and just do something spontaneous, actually enjoy myself. Cara looked at me eagerly, and I was pretty sure she was holding her breath in anticipation of my answer.

I sighed heavily as my eyes looked over around the barren room. "Where are we going?" I asked. Cara squealed and looped her arms around my neck, nearly knocking me off-balance.

"This is going to be so much fun!" She pulled back, and her eyes danced down my body. "But you need to change. This dress is a little much for where we're going. Throw on some jeans and a T-shirt."

I groaned but turned to dig through my boxes for an outfit that looked like hers. With clothes in hand, I turned back around to see Cara sitting on the edge of my bed.

"Can I have a minute?"

"What? You have something under that dress that I've never seen before? Because if you have a dick, I've already been there, done that." She rolled her eyes and tossed my sweat pants toward the pile of boxes. She laughed as my eyes widened from her crass comment.

I chewed my lip as I turned my back to Cara so she wouldn't see me turn pink again. Pulling my blue sundress over my head, I was wondering if I'd regret my decision to go out with her. I'd never had many friends, so I wasn't comfortable undressing in front of anyone, but I wasn't going to make myself look any more naïve than I already had. Besides, my paisley bra and underwear covered as much as a bikini would.

"Wow, you have a killer body, Ellie. I'm envious. I have to say, I expected granny panties under there to hide the stick in your ass."

I let out a small laugh. Someone as beautiful as Cara saying they were envious of me was ridiculous. I stepped into my jeans and wiggled them up over my hips. "Come on. I saw you in nothing but a towel, and we both know you have nothing to be envious of. Oh, and I don't have a stick up my ass."

"Oh my God. I bet that was the first curse word you've ever said!"

I glanced over my shoulder and narrowed my eyes at her. "I'm a nice person, not a *fucking* robot," I replied, and now it was she who was shocked.

"I'll have to stay between you and Tristan tonight."

"Who's Tristan?" I asked as I pulled my shirt on and turned to face her. She got up from the bed and walked toward me. Her hands slid on either side of my neck as she pulled my long hair from under my gray shirt before slipping her fingers under the delicate chain of my mother's necklace and pulling it out as well.

"Tristan is my boyfriend." Her face lit up as she looked me over with approval. "But he has some really good-looking friends, and they will be fighting to get their dirty hands on you," she added with a wink before taking my hand and pulling me toward the bedroom door.

"Wait," I slid my feet into my sandals before letting her pull me out into the hall. We tiptoed our way to the stairs, pausing whenever one creaked beneath our feet. When we reached the bottom, we both made a dash for the front door, struggling to suppress our giggles.

Sitting at the end of the driveway was a dark car that was already running, but its headlights were turned off.

I shook my head at Cara as her smirk grew. "You're a bad influence."

"Maybe. But you're a good influence, so I need you. You can't back out now, Ellie. I'm tired of only hanging out with guys." Her bottom lip jutted out in a mock pout, and all I could do was laugh as I was practically dragged down the porch steps to the waiting vehicle.

Cara pulled open the passenger door, and the driver smiled, revealing dimples in his sun-kissed skin. He was the male version of Cara: breathtaking. Tugging at my tank top, I looked down to the ground.

"I'm Tristan," he said, his blue eyes sparkling as he ran his hand over his sandy brown hair that was a few inches long on top, but shaved shorter on the sides. It was dark, but he looked a few years older than us, and I wondered how they met.

"This is Ellie." Cara bent down and slid across the bench seat, not releasing my hand, forcing me to sit next to her.

"I could sit in the back," I mumbled as we pulled out into the dark street.

"The guys will be sitting back there, and I can't let you alone with them on your first night out." She reached forward and turned up the radio as I stared out the passenger window, my hand still in her grasp.

"Ellie...is that short for Elizabeth?" Tristan asked, glancing around Cara.

"Elise, actually. I was named after my father's great-grandmother." I replied, averting my gaze from his mesmerizing blue eyes. He was almost too handsome to look at.

"I'm going to call you El," Cara said as if she was just thinking out loud.

"So Tristan, did you go to school with Cara?"

"Nah, I'm in college. I go to U Dub."

"I'll be going there in a few months," Cara said. Tristan didn't know that she was going to still be in high school next year? I wondered what else she had lied to him about.

"What about you?" Tristan turned down a street to our left.

"Umm...I'm not really sure. Plans change." I stared out of the passenger window, begging myself to keep my tears at bay. I was supposed to start college after senior year, but after my mother's accident, I needed to get a job and my own place. I had no intention of staying at David's for any longer than necessary. I wasn't completely opposed to having my father in my life. In fact, it was something I'd always dreamed about when I was younger, but I didn't want it to be like this. I wanted him to want to be my parent and not be forced to step up to the plate.

I lived only an hour from Blackwell, but it felt like a completely different world than I'd been raised in. My mother had grown her own vegetable garden, and she spent her evenings off with me. We lived in a modest two-bedroom apartment, but it was plenty of room for just the two of us.

My father's house seemed to be designed to make sure the occupants didn't have to interact unless absolutely necessary. The thought made me sad, like most of my thoughts lately.

After a few minutes of silence, I tried to make small talk. "So where are we going?"

Cara and Tristan looked at each other and laughed. "Don't freak out"—Cara cleared her throat—"but we're going to hit a frat party."

"You're not serious," I groaned. The car made a sudden right turn, and we drove down a long dirt driveway. *I can handle this.* "This doesn't look like a party." My eyes narrowed as I looked over the darkened house at the end of the lane, and my heartbeat seemed to slow. This wasn't so bad.

"Not here. We're just picking up Luke, Cameron, and Brody."

"Great," I mumbled as three guys came out of the shadows of the wraparound porch. As they stepped in front of the headlights, I had to swallow back the lump in my throat. They were all tall, muscular, and every bit as handsome as Tristan. *What do they put in the drinking water around here?*

"Cameron is the taller one with dark hair, and Luke and Brody are brothers."

My eyes danced over the three men. I could definitely pick out the brother who had dirty-blond hair. One had a sleeve of tattoos, and the other didn't have any that I could see.

Cameron pulled open the back door and slid into the backseat, placing his large hand on Cara's shoulder next to me. *He smells incredible.*

"Who's your friend, Cara?" he asked with a deep, husky voice. The other two guys slid into the seat on either side of him and the doors closed, causing the overhead light to go off. I was thankful they could no longer see how pink my cheeks were.

"This is my girl, El. She just moved in with me." She squeezed my hand reassuringly, and I relaxed a little. I was never good around groups of people. I usually kept to myself, my face buried in a book. Social interaction wasn't my strong suit.

"Nice to meet you," the deep voice called out. "I'm Cameron." I turned to look at him over my shoulder. His eyes were dark like mine. His hair was chestnut brown and cut short all over but still managed to look messy.

"Nice to meet you," I nodded before turning back forward.

"The other two are Luke and Brody. You'll have to forget their rudeness," Cara said as her voice rose, cutting into their private conversation in the back.

"Sorry. El, is it? Nice to meet you," one of them replied.

"It's about time Cara started bringing some girls around." The other laughed, and she turned to glare at him. "Getting tired of hanging out with all these assholes all the time."

"It doesn't make a difference, Brody, because El isn't into douchebags." Cara gave me a side glance as she tried to stifle a laugh. I was glad she was standing up for me. Maybe this party wouldn't be so bad.

We drove for another fifteen minutes while the radio blared and the guys sang off-key.

"What's that smell?" A cloud of smoke enveloped my head from behind, and someone laughed.

"It's just pot," Cara whispered as a hand came between our faces holding a small silver pipe.

"Cara," I groaned between gritted teeth as her hand left mine. She took the small pipe. A second later a lighter was passed up to her, and she placed the device between her lips and held the lighter to the bowl end.

"C'mere," she choked out as she tried to hold her breath.

I leaned closer to her as one of the guys from behind us said, "Fuck, yeah. They're gonna make out." *Was she really going to kiss me?*

"Stop being gay, Cam," Tristan called out, and Cara flinched at his choice of words.

"How does it make me gay to watch two girls?" he asked, offended that his manhood was being challenged, whatever that meant. "That doesn't even make any fucking sense."

"First of all, my girlfriend won't be doing nothing with another girl unless I'm between them. And you damn sure won't be watching, *Bingo*." His tone was not playful in the slightest, and it made me stiffen. I wanted to ask why he'd called him Bingo, but after his outburst, it didn't feel like a good idea.

I glared behind me as Cara grabbed my chin to keep me facing her. "Breathe in." As the words left her lips, thick white smoke rolled from her mouth. I inhaled as much as I could. "Hold it in."

I struggled to hold my breath, but my chest began to burn, and as I exhaled I coughed and sputtered. The guys began to laugh, but Cara tucked my hair behind my ear, concern in her eyes. "Are you all right?"

"I'm fine." *Just a little humiliated.* My head began to feel light, and the feeling soon spread throughout my body. Cara passed the pipe to Tristan who lit it by himself as he pressed his knee against the bottom of the steering wheel to keep us on the road. Normally I would have freaked out, but I felt too good to care. It was the first time in days that I wasn't upset, and I just kept telling myself that I deserved this.

We pulled up to a large two-story home with people standing all around the front lawn, drinks in hand. The bass from the music was so loud I felt it vibrate through my body. I looked to Cara, who gave me a small smile before I opened the passenger door and stepped out onto the road. Cara slid out behind me and clutched my hand in hers. I immediately relaxed at her touch.

"It's going to be fun, but if you don't like it, we can leave," she assured me as she began to pull me toward Tristan.

Brody groaned at the mention of leaving. "I will make it my personal mission to make sure you have fun, because I am for damn sure not going home until I am too drunk to remember my own name, or someone is moaning it."

"Charming," I mumbled to myself as we crossed the street and walked up the sidewalk to the front door. As we entered, I kept my head ducked. The guys all yelled to their friends, and the partygoers seemed pleased at their arrival. I wanted to melt into the wall, and with my buzz, I felt like that might actually be possible.

CHAPTER SIX

Cara

As we slipped into the house, I kept El close by my side. I could feel her grip tighten as we became submerged in the crowd.

"We're going to have fun, I promise." I gave her hand a quick squeeze back, and she smiled, her shoulders relaxing.

"I'm not really good with lots of people," she whispered as if someone might overhear her.

"I'm better in crowds than I am alone," I confessed with a smirk, but her eyebrows pulled together, trying to understand. "I don't like to be alone with my thoughts." I tapped at my head with my free hand. "Lots of scary things going on up there," I added with a wink, eliciting a giggle from her. *She laughs like Tatum.*

"I'm going to grab a drink," Tristan called over the music, pulling my attention from Ellie.

"Sure," I gave him a smile as he bent down and placed a chaste kiss on the corner of my mouth. The other guys followed him, leaving me with Ellie.

"You want to explore or something?" I asked as someone ran behind me, knocking me slightly off-balance. "Whoa! What the hell?" I spun around to see Ally, her arms crossed over her chest and a smirk on her lips.

"Oops," she shrugged as if it was an innocent mistake, her eyes narrowing as she glanced behind me to El. "Is this your new replacement for Tristan?" My body stiffened at her words, because I already knew that El was the perfect package. I relaxed my face so she wouldn't see my insecurities.

"Just because he doesn't want you, it doesn't mean he is going to leave me, Ally."

"I'm the one who doesn't want him, Cara, and we both know why. Don't say I didn't warn you." She raised her eyebrow before disappearing through the crowd. I took a deep breath and turned back to El, doing my best to smile convincingly.

"So…want to explore?"

"Yeah, sure." She looked like she had a million questions, and I knew I'd have to answer a few.

"Come on." I kept hold of her hand as I pulled her through the crowd toward a set of stairs just inside the entryway. I grabbed the banister and made my way toward the top, stepping over a couple who were practically fucking, sprawled out on the stairs.

"That's going to leave some bruises." I laughed, and El covered her mouth with her other hand to muffle her own giggle. I pulled her hand free from her face.

"It's nice to hear you laugh after everything that's happened to you. Don't hide it on account of those perverts."

We made our way to the top landing and glanced around at all of the closed doors. One popped open, and I grabbed my chest, startled.

"Bathroom's all yours," he called out to us as he walked by and down the stairs.

"I guess we start with the bathroom," I shrugged and pulled her toward the darkened area. I flicked on the light and screamed, jumping back into El as my eyes landed on the couple in the tub, his white ass rising and falling on top of a redhead on all fours.

Doubling over in laughter, I flicked off the light. "My bad," I called out as I pulled the door closed. El was bent over, making an odd yipping sound as she struggled to catch her breath. "Bet they didn't have that in your porn book."

Her hand flew out, hitting me in the stomach as she finally managed to calm herself down. I reached up and wiped happy tears from her eyes.

"What do you think is behind door number two?" she asked, and I bit my lip, suppressing my smile as I took her hand and pulled her to the next door.

"Do you want to do the honors?"

"It would be my pleasure." She laughed as she gripped the brass knob in her hand and turned it. Behind it was another sexual adventure, but this was two girls making out on a bed as a guy nearby watched, jerking off. His brow was furrowed in concentration as a girl with a short blond bob ran her tongue over a brunette's nipple, causing it to harden.

He glanced our way, unfazed by the interruption. In fact, he seemed pleased to see us. "There's room for two more," he said, his hand working against himself as he looked us over.

"No, thank you," El called out in the most polite voice she could manage, pulling the door closed. The look on her face was priceless, as if she'd just witnessed the most horrific act of her life.

"Two girls was a little much, huh?"

El shook her head as her eyes met mine. "His thing was so…little."

I burst out laughing as I pulled her away from the door. "His *thing*? It's called a dick, and yes, it was frighteningly small."

"Good thing the guys weren't up here to see that, huh? Tristan seemed a little…" She let her words trail off as she looked up at me.

"Tristan is a small-town boy. Small town, small mind." I made a face, embarrassed by the way they spoke around Ellie. But part of me was pleased that she found what they said offensive. As sheltered as she seemed, she wasn't close minded. *Would you judge me if you found out about my past?*

"Speaking of which, who was that girl?"

"She used to date Tristan. Her friends all treated me like shit when I got here. He didn't like it, so he left her. A few weeks later, he asked me out." I shrugged. "She spread a bunch of nasty rumors about him after that. It was awful."

"I think I need a drink."

"Let's go find the guys and get us a little liquored up before we check out any more doors." I looped my arm in El's as we made our way back down the steps to the entryway. I turned to walk us through the living room, which was packed with people dancing and Christmas lights flashing. El stopped walking, pulling me to a halt.

"How are we going to get through all of those people?" she asked as I began to walk again, tugging her with me.

"Just shake your ass, and we'll shimmy our way through. Just don't let go of my hand." I unlooped my arm and slid my fingers in hers, giving her a reassuring squeeze.

"There he is," I yelled over my shoulder to her as I spotted Tristan in the kitchen, a Solo cup at his mouth.

CHAPTER SEVEN
Ellie

I kept close behind Cara as we wove our way through the rooms. Once we reached the kitchen, Tristan poured us each a drink. When I went to take the cup he held onto it, his eyes locked on mine. He was the perfect person to be with Cara—both devastatingly beautiful. It made me uncomfortable to hold eye contact with him even for a few seconds. His gaze was too intense, and it caused a chill to run down my spine.

"Don't take a drink from anyone but me or Cara, understand?"

I nodded, and his fingers slid from the cup as Cara looked at me and rolled her eyes, gulping down the contents of hers in one swallow.

I drank down my liquor, my throat immediately in flames from the harsh taste. I made a face, and Cara laughed as she took my cup and handed them both back to Tristan.

"Slow down," he warned her quietly before his stern look turned to me, but he refilled our cups for us again. *Was he always this serious?*

"We need to catch up," Cara replied as she winked toward me.

Brody, Luke, and Cameron got drinks for themselves and went their own ways as Tristan struck up a conversation with some guy wearing a blue T-shirt with yellow Greek letters across the chest. Cara pulled me away, laughing as she took a sip from her cup.

"Isn't this fun?"

My eyes scanned over the room full of bodies dancing to the mindless beat. I shrugged, unsure of how I fit in with this crowd. "It's…different."

"Come on, let loose a little." She pulled me toward the center of the room, and I set my cup down on a stand beside the couch as we disappeared into the masses. Cara's hand left mine, and she held both her arms over her head as she swayed her hips to the beat. I began to move with her. Even though I wasn't one for parties, I loved to dance. Judging by the look on Cara's face, she was pleased by my moves. I turned around, and her hands grabbed my hips, pulling my back against her chest as a scene I read from my book played through my head.

We danced together through three full songs until our bodies were slick with sweat, but I didn't care. I wanted to keep going. I noticed Tristan with his back against the far wall, watching us as he drank from his cup, his jaw clenched with what looked like frustration.

Brody was at his side, and he said something to Tristan before his eyes were on us, too, as we moved.

I began to sway my hips more, bending at my knees as I moved against Cara. It was odd feeling like the center of attention, but I knew this was probably how Cara felt all of the time. She was very outgoing, and I had always wished it was that easy for me to let go and not care what others thought.

"I think Brody likes you," Cara spoke into my ear. I watched as Brody's eyes traveled up and down my body before shaking my head. "Let's give him a show."

"I think he just likes watching two girls grind on the dance floor." I brushed off the idea, but it didn't stop me from pushing my ass back against her a little harder.

"Oh come on. You must realize how freaking hot you are." Cara moved her hands to my shoulders and spun me around to face her. "Brody is practically ready to fuck you right here. Go ask him to dance."

"What? No! I don't even know him. We just met today."

"*We* just met the other day, too, but you're out here with *me*." She cocked her eyebrow and crossed her arms over her chest. Her words struck me. Why was I so willing to follow Cara blindly through all of this? What was it about her that made me feel secure? *You're different.* "Come on. Any girl here would be dying to fuck that man's face."

"You included?" I laughed as I looked over my shoulder to Brody, who took a drink from his beer bottle before licking his lips. *Why are you trying so hard to push me on Brody when we are having so much fun together?*

"No," she replied quietly. I glanced back at her before looking back to Brody. "I'd be over there admiring you, if I wasn't the one lucky enough to already be dancing with you." Every nerve ending in my body seemed to fire off at once with her words. How could someone as beautiful as Cara really think of me as attractive?

My gaze drifted over his muscular tattooed arm as a blush crept over my cheeks from her words. "He's trouble." I shook my head as I studied the tribal swirls that covered his flesh.

"One kiss from that man, and we might be able to dislodge that stick you have jammed up your ass."

"Again, I do not have *anything* jammed up my ass, as you so eloquently put it, and I need some air." With this many bodies packed into such a small room, it was becoming hard to breathe, and this conversation wasn't helping.

I slipped by Cara and made my way to the kitchen and out the back door, feeling humiliated. There was a small porch, and there was surprisingly no one lingering around the back of the house. I sat down on the edge of the top step as the door opened behind me. I didn't have to look to know it was Cara.

"I'm a fucking idiot," she said as she sat down next to me with a sigh.

"You're in good company," I joked as she rolled her eyes and ran her fingers through her long hair. *I'm the fucking idiot.*

"You've never even *kissed* a boy?"

"Of course I've *kissed* a boy, just not…you know… *kissed* one." I could feel my cheeks burning red with embarrassment. Cara slipped her hand in mine and gave it a squeeze.

"Why are you blushing? It's *not* a big deal. Any of those idiots in the party would be happy to kiss you. If you don't like Brody, we can find someone else. You're a hottie."

"Who says I *want* to kiss them?" I asked with a sarcastic laugh, our gaze meeting. I hated that I was feeling so conflicted inside. I longed for the protective bubble that I grew up in where I didn't need to entertain these feelings. "I just don't want the first time to be humiliating in front of a crowd of people."

Cara's brow creased slightly before she swallowed, her tongue running out over her lower lip as her gaze dipped to my mouth. "Do you trust me?"

I laughed, shaking my head slightly. "No. I don't even know you."

The sides of her mouth turned up in a smile as her head tilted to the side. "We can change that." She winked, and I couldn't help but smile; I dug my teeth into my lip as my butterflies began to take flight in my stomach. Even I was drawn to Cara's beauty, but my clouded brain told me her flirtatious behavior was a direct result of weed and liquor. When I didn't respond, she took matters into her own hands.

"Fine," she sighed dramatically as she put her hands on either side of my face. "I'll show you how to do it, but you have to promise not to tell any of those idiots in there, or they will make us do it all the time, like circus monkeys." But as she spoke I knew she was more worried about their judgment, and then it dawned on me what was going to happen next.

"Wait…what? No, Cara. I'm not going to kiss—" my words were cut off as Cara's soft lips pressed against mine. *Fuck.* She pulled back fractionally and angled her head to the left as her mouth moved tenderly against mine. Her tongue slid over my lower lip, and I sighed, my lips parting slightly to grant her access.

"Just do what I'm doing," she whispered before our tongues met. My hands instinctively went to her neck. *I need you closer.* I could feel her touch tingle through my body all the way to my toes. Our mouths pressed a little harder, our tongues pushed a little deeper as our chests brushed. My body was on fire, and I couldn't believe I was scared of something that came so naturally.

Cara pulled back, and I slowly opened my eyes as a smile spread across her face. "Not bad, huh?"

I nodded like an idiot, because I had no idea how to respond to what had just happened. She stood, brushing off the backside of her jeans before holding out her hand and pulling me to my feet, and I wobbled.

"You're right about not wanting to kiss any of those idiots in there. I don't blame you." She turned to walk to the back door, and as she pulled it open, she called out over her shoulder, "You're welcome, El."

"I didn't thank you for sexually assaulting me, Cara." But I wanted to thank her, I was just too embarrassed, and her kiss left me with a high much more potent than anything I'd consumed tonight.

She reached behind her, and I slipped my hand in hers as we went back inside the house, making our way to the living room. Cara scanned the room for Tristan. He stumbled out of the hallway that led back behind the stairs with a red plastic cup in his hand.

"Babe, where the hell did you guys go? I was worried. You know you shouldn't wander around these parties alone." His words sounded concerned, but there was an edge to his tone, a warning. Guilt and shame washed over me. *I wonder if anyone saw Cara kiss me.*

"I wasn't alone." She held up our clasped hands, and I struggled to suppress my giggle. Clearly, she wasn't concerned.

His eyes were glazed over, but his lips twisted in a smile as he pulled Cara against his chest, his hand on her ass as he kissed her as she and I had just done moments before, only with more force. She held on to my hand, and I stood there awkwardly as they made out. I grabbed the cup from Tristan's other hand and drank the contents as I waited for them to come up for air.

I gulped down the drink as a heavy arm went around my shoulders, and I jumped, looking up at a smiling Brody.

"Did you save a dance for me?" he asked, winking his honey-colored eye.

"Actually, I'm taking a breather." I shrugged his arm off my shoulders and took a small step away from him. *Did I really prefer to stand here and watch Tristan shove his tongue down her throat?*

The corners of his mouth fought against a smile as he raised his beer bottle to his lips. "Breathing Cara's air?" he whispered as he cocked his eyebrow and took a drink from his beer. My eyes widened, and I pulled my hand free from Cara's.

"I'm going to go dance with Brody," I announced to absolutely no one; Tristan had all of her attention. I shoved the cup back in Tristan's hand with a frustrated groan.

Brody put his arm around my waist and guided me back toward the living room. We stopped in the middle of the room, and I put my hands against his chest to put some space between us. "What did you mean by that comment?" *Please tell me you didn't see us.*

"Well, unless you were choking and in desperate need of mouth-to-mouth, I'd say you were making out with Tristan's girlfriend. I'm not judging. It was fucking hot." *This was bad, this was so bad.*

I could feel my face burn with embarrassment. I opened and closed my mouth several times, unable to form a coherent response. *How will I talk my way out of this?*

"Are you choking now? Because I'd be more than happy to give you a little assistance myself." He placed his large hands on my sides and dipped his head closer to mine.

What would Cara do? I glanced back toward where I'd left her. Cara would shove her tongue down his throat and shut him up, but that was the last thing I wanted to do.

"Well?" he asked, his gaze dropping to my mouth as he licked his lips.

"You're not my type."

"You mean I don't have tits, right?"

I stiffened my back and tried my best to look confident as I folded my arms across my chest. "Are you jealous, Brody?"

He looked thrown off-guard as if he'd expected a different response. I was actually shocked myself that I had said it. But I didn't regret kissing Cara; in fact, it was all that was running through my mind. She was so confident, and her entire persona radiated sexiness.

"Absolutely." He flashed his perfect white smile, and I nearly dissolved into a puddle on the floor. I was quickly jostled back to reality as someone dancing bumped into me from behind, causing me to fall against Brody's toned chest. His arms slid around my back, holding me against him to steady me.

"You okay?" he asked, his tone no longer flirtatious, only concerned.

I nodded, trying to pull back, but he kept his grip firm.

"Have I earned that dance yet, or are you going to make me beg?"

I raked my teeth over my bottom lip before I began to move my hips like I had when I was dancing with Cara. Brody began to move with me, and I was surprised at how well he danced. His hands slid against my back, leaving a trail of want in his wake.

"You're not bad," I called out as I put my hands around his neck.

"Oh, I'm very, very bad."

I laughed out loud at his cocky response, relaxing in his arms as the song changed and the crowd cheered. We continued to dance, my body grinding hard against his as the alcohol lowered my inhibitions more. I could feel how much Brody was enjoying this, too, as his length pressed against my hip. I turned around in his arms, pressing my bottom against him, and he groaned approvingly in my ear, his liquor-laced breath fanning over my cheek. His fingers roamed over my ribs before his hand pressed against my belly, pulling me tighter against him.

As much as I was enjoying getting lost in the moment, I knew I was taking this new carefree attitude too far too fast.

"I'm going to grab my drink," I spoke over the booming music as I turned to face him. He nodded, and his hand went to the small of my back as I worked my way through the other partygoers. I grabbed my cup I'd sat on the stand beside the couch and gulped down the last sip.

Brody set down his empty bottle and took my cup. "Let's get some refills."

I followed him into the kitchen were several guys were tossing ping-pong balls into cups on either side of the table. Luke was leaning against the counter with his arms around the waist of a very inebriated blonde. He nodded to his brother as he looked to me, his smile growing. Brody just shook his head at his brother's teasing.

"What did you have in here?" he asked turning to face me.

"Um…it tasted like one of those hot candies." I thought of the taste still lingering on Cara's tongue as it slid over mine.

"Fireball. You came to party." He nodded his head once with approval. I turned my attention to the crowd around the table as everyone yelled. Someone was forced to gulp down a drink. "Here," Brody's arm came over my shoulder from behind, and my eyes danced over the intricate tribal tattoo that left barely any flesh to be seen.

"Thank you," I took the cup and continued to watch the game unfold as Brody's arm slid around my waist, and he leaned back against the counter, pulling me back against him.

"So why'd you move in with Cara?" he asked. I closed my eyes, willing the sad memories to stay away. This wasn't the time to grieve or relive the kiss on the porch that was running through my mind on instant replay.

"She lives with my father."

"Really? It's weird we've never seen you around here before."

I sighed. "I grew up in Haleford, Georgia." I took a drink, and the crowd erupted again in front of us. I was thankful to the interruption to our conversation. Brody was a good-looking guy, but I wasn't trying to give my life story to anyone here. This was my chance to be someone new.

"How old are you?" I asked, my eyes still fixed ahead.

"I'll be twenty in a month. You?"

"Eighteen," I lied, knowing they already thought Cara was legally an adultas well, not that they cared, seeing that they were serving us alcohol.

CHAPTER EIGHT

Cara

I pulled back from Tristan, catching my breath from our passionate kiss. He smirked as he slid his thumb across my lower lip, the evidence of his happiness still pressed against my hip. But all I could think about was the softness in Ellie's kiss. Tristan was anything but tender. *What the hell is wrong with me?* I had acted without regard for the repercussions, and even though I didn't regret it, I was worried she might. I might have destroyed a friendship with her before it even had a chance to begin. My stomach twisted in knots at the idea. And what might be something innocent among some friends now left me feeling guilty that I'd betrayed Tristan. I knew he wouldn't see it as harmless if he ever found out.

I glanced around us, and I realized I'd let Ellie wander around the party by herself. She was never going to talk to me again unless she was already avoiding me.

"Shit. I need to find El."

"What is it with that girl? She seems a little uptight."

"She's not uptight, she's just not used to letting go." I replied as I laced my fingers in his and pulled him through the crowd. He tugged on my hand, making me stop and look back at him.

"Let her have some fun. Maybe we can slip off into a room for a few minutes." His eyes narrowed playfully as he pulled me back toward him.

I shook my head as I backed away. "I have to make sure she's okay. She's going through a hard time. Her mom just died, and she doesn't have anyone. She doesn't even really know David."

His smile faded, and he nodded. I was thankful in that moment that he was so understanding. Tristan had always been protective and caring, even if he tried to hide it behind his college partier persona. He was rebelling against his conservative parents, but the core values they had taught him were still there, hidden under layers of indifference, often making me feel guilty that I no longer believed in anything.

"You have a lot in common with her, huh?" His voice was low, quiet.

I could only nod, swallowing back the lump in my throat. My mother was very much alive, and it was I who was dead to her. But that past was too muddy to drag Tristan through, so I told him she was gone and let him draw his own conclusions.

It wasn't a lie, I told myself. I was only responsible for my words, not for how they were interpreted.

"Maybe bringing her here wasn't such a good idea. I swear sometime you don't think…" And as he spoke, I knew that hidden under his kind eyes I was being scolded. He was right. Why would I think this would make things better for her when none of it helped me? But then I remembered that it was his idea to invite her along, and my guilt turned to frustration.

I turned, unable to be under the judgmental gaze of his blue eyes, and wove my way through the dancers in the living room. I spotted Ellie in the kitchen with Brody, alleviating some of my guilt.

"He doesn't strike me as her type," Tristan commented just as Ellie's gaze found us.

"Why are you always so hard on Bro? He's a good guy and one of your closest friends." I looked at the way Brody held her.

"He's a user, and he's going to break your friend's heart. Don't say I didn't warn you."

"Consider me warned," I rolled my eyes as I walked toward them. I was growing tired of the alpha-male bullshit.

CHAPTER NINE
Ellie

"You having fun?" Cara asked with a giggle as her eyes went from Brody to me.

"It's all right." I shrugged, and she winked in response. *Why did that tiny gesture send shivers through my body?*

"You need a drink?" Tristan asked Cara. She nodded in response before he looked to me.

"I have one." I held up my cup as he tilted his head to the side before scratching the back of his head. I realized I'd already broken the rule of letting someone else get me a drink. He kissed Cara on the temple and poured out their new drinks.

"We call next," Cara shouted above the guys playing in front of us.

"You're not serious." *Please don't add public humiliation to the list of new experiences tonight.*

"Come on, El. All you have to do is get the ball in the cup. It's easy. Bro and Tris can be a team."

"I'm down," Brody responded, and Tristan nodded once as he held out Cara's drink for her to take.

We watched the rest of the game, and I studied what the players did so I wouldn't look like I was completely new to everything that was going on. I was a quick learner and regardless of what Cara said, fairly good at concealing my true self. I could blend and become one of them, live my life vicariously through Cara.

I stood next to Cara, ping-pong ball in hand as I lined up my shot. I tossed it, and it bounced off Tristan's chest, which rumbled with laughter.

"Okay, so I suck." I shrugged as I rolled my eyes.

"I can let you practice handling my balls if you think it will help," Brody said with a laugh as Tristan's arm hit him across the chest.

"Don't be a dick," Tristan growled, and I couldn't help but smile.

"Get your mind out of the gutter, Bro," Cara snapped, and my eyes went to him as his smirk disappeared behind his bottle of beer. I loved that they were looking out for me, but behind the crude humor, I could tell Brody was just playing around. I think he enjoyed pushing Tristan's buttons.

I picked up the cup of beer and downed it, wiping a drop on my chin with the back of my hand. We continued to play, and the crowd around us grew as we all became more inebriated. I was feeling no pain, and finally, the memories of the last week were safely hidden in the back of my mind. I'd done it—been able to slip away and find some semblance of enjoyment. Cara and I lost our game, but we began a friendship that I knew would be crucial in my ability to move forward in life.

We played another round before slipping back into the living room, and the four of us danced together in a group. The music pulsed through my body as Christmas lights that hung along the walls twinkled in rainbow colors. During the daylight hours this place would probably look uninhabitable, but in the late hours of the night, it was transformed. I couldn't wipe the grin from my face, even in the intense heat of swaying bodies.

Brody's hands roamed over my thighs, igniting a fire in my veins that I never knew had sparked. I rested the back of my head against his chest, exhausted but not wanting the night to end.

"I need some air," Brody mumbled into my hair, as I stifled a yawn. My eyes looked around us, and I realized that only a few people remained dancing. Most were making out or passed out.

I looked to Cara, who nodded, and we all headed out to the back porch. I hoped Brody wouldn't bring up what he'd witnessed out here earlier, but he was more concerned with getting high.

"You want to hit the blunt?" He held out a brown cigar that looked homemade. I nodded as he lit it, and the familiar smell from the car engulfed us.

He held it out between us, and I took it, nearly dropping it on my jeans. Looking out at the darkened yard, I pressed my lips to the end and inhaled, waiting for the burn to settle in my chest. I quickly exhaled before I began to cough and held it out to Cara, who sat down on the first step, nestled between Tristan's thighs.

I ran my tongue over my lower lip, tasting the lingering strawberry flavor from the cigar wrapping. Brody slid his leg around me, and I leaned back against his chest as I looked up at the twinkling stars in the night sky.

"Ah! Did you see that? It was a shooting star!" Cara sat straight up, a wide grin across her face as she pointed out into the abyss.

"Make a wish," Brody replied to her from behind me.

"She's already got me. What more does she need?" Tristan laughed as he exhaled his hit of weed.

"The Japanese believe that if you make a thousand paper cranes, you will be granted one wish," I mumbled. After a few seconds Brody began laughing, his chest rumbling against the back of my head. I sat up and turned to look over my shoulder. "What?"

"It just seems easier to wish on a star. Seriously. That's a lot of fucking paper. Think of the trees, new girl." He laughed so hard he began to cough, and Cara giggled uncontrollably to the point her face was red.

"Not to mention the time it would take." Tristan passed the blunt to Brody.

"Some things are worth the effort." I shrugged before leaning back against Brody's toned chest, his tattooed arm sliding around my stomach.

"Brody likes his wishes like he likes his women… easy!" Cara doubled over, but her laughter no longer made a sound as she slapped her thigh.

"Well, he's sitting with the wrong girl then," I huffed as I took the blunt from Brody's thick fingers. "It was just something my mom told me." I shrugged and looked back to the sky. Cara's laughter abruptly ended, and a silence fell between us.

"Don't listen to them about me. I am definitely sitting with the right girl," he whispered into my ear, causing goose bumps to spread like wildfire across my flesh.

On the ride back to our home in the early morning hours, I rested my head against Cara's shoulder as her fingers twisted in my hair. The back seat now only had Cameron's long body stretched across it as he slept.

Luke had wandered off to one of the bedrooms in the frat house with some random chick, and Brody wasn't ready to end the party. I tried not to show my disappointment when he decided not to leave with us. Cara had warned me he wasn't the boyfriend type; I should just have fun, and the right person would find me.

I pulled my legs up to my chest and let my eyes flutter closed as we made our way back home. Tristan dropped us off at the end of the driveway. He was going back to Cameron's to crash for the night. He waited at the end of the lane until we were safely inside before leaving.

Sneaking back into the house was more frightening than when we'd left, and I wasn't sure if it was paranoia induced by the weed. Cara wouldn't stop giggling, and I had to squeeze her hand repeatedly to quiet her down. Even if we did get caught, it would have been worth it. Those couple of hours just being part of the crowd and leaving my old life behind had meant the world to me.

As we reached the top of the stairs, Cara fell against her door causing her to lapse into a fit of giggles that only made the slightest squeaking sound before she snorted loudly. I turned her doorknob, causing her to nearly trip over her own feet before guiding her to her bed. She fell back on to her pillow, pulling me down with her, her dark hair splayed out over the rich fabric. I pushed myself off her, my face burning with embarrassment.

I pulled off her sneakers as she wiggled her toes beneath rainbow-striped socks.

"Good night," I whispered entirely too loudly and turned to leave her room.

"El," Cara called out, and I turned to look at her. "I want you to teach me how to make paper cranes." She turned on her side and curled into a ball with her hand under her pillow, and I couldn't wipe the smile from my face. *Tonight had been perfect.*

"Okay," I slipped out of her room and pulled her door closed behind me, carefully tiptoeing to my room. Once inside, I let out a sigh of relief that we hadn't gotten caught, even though it would have been worth it. Sliding out of my sandals, I stripped out of my jeans and fell back on my bed, letting the memories of the night wash over me as I drifted off into sleep.

CHAPTER TEN
Cara

After lying in the dark silence for a few moments, I got up from my bed and flipped open the laptop on my dresser as I hummed my favorite song. I typed "paper crane" into the search engine and pulled up an instructional video on origami.

Taking a piece of paper from my notebook, I ripped it from the binding and began to drunkenly fold the paper over and over until I was left with something that resembled a throwing star, far from a magical bird that could grant wishes. *Fuck.*

I crumbled the paper and tossed it on the floor before typing Ellie's name into the search engine. I clicked on recent stories and covered my mouth with my palm when I saw the link that explained the tragic death of her mother, a shooting victim of a convenience store robbery.

My eyes danced over the screen as I struggled with the morality of learning of her past from the Internet instead of just having the guts to ask her. David didn't want to talk about what had happened to his ex, like if he didn't explain the past, then it never happened. That's why we never discussed how I had come to live with them.

Sighing, I closed my laptop and padded back to my bed, stripping off my clothes along the way so by the time I fell onto my bed, I was wearing nothing but yellow panties.

I crawled under my quilt and stared up at the dark ceiling as I struggled to get my mind to shut off. Nighttime was always hard for me when I was alone.

When I couldn't hold my eyes open any longer, I drifted off in a restless sleep, plagued by images of the party. I pictured Ellie, looking horrified as I kissed her, her hand coming down hard across my face. The sound of her slap caused everyone to stop and look at us, and we were now in the center of the room as they pointed and laughed at me.

I could actually feel the painful burn on my cheek all the way down into my chest, where my heart ached with humiliation and regret.

I shoved my way through the crowd of people and pulled open the front door, but I was not met with the freedom of being able to run away again. Instead I was face-to-face with my mother, her tearstained face only inches from mine. *Please don't cry.*

"I regret you," she whispered, venom in her tone.

I shoved her to the side and slipped out into the cold night air, running barefoot down the road as the stones bit into the flesh of my heels. My sob echoed in the trees around me, and I was now lost in a forest, afraid and cold in the middle of the night. I could no longer hear the yells of those who disapproved, but my own sobs mocked me as they played back in my ears. It was myself that I was most afraid of.

I dropped to my knees, sinking into the moist soil, slowly letting it encapsulate me. I didn't begin to struggle until it reached my chest, and the suppression of breathing sparked a panic inside of me. But I had no one left to hear my screams. I was fighting alone, against myself.

My pleas for help slowly turned into a melodic song, but the sound was muffled, and I struggled to hear my own voice amid the rustling of the leaves.

My eyes shot open, and I wiped them, still able to hear the song in my head. I sat up, wiping the sleep from my eyes as I realized the sound was actually coming from the other side of my bedroom wall.

Tiptoeing over next to my headboard, I pressed my ear against the cold wall and listened to the music that Ellie was using to lull her to sleep.

"Hey," I whispered loudly and tapped against the wall. After a moment, I tapped again.

"Sorry," Ellie whispered back, and I smiled.

"No, don't be. It's nice. Good night," I whispered before crawling back under my covers and drifting off to sleep.

CHAPTER ELEVEN

Ellie

Morning came too soon, and for once I didn't want to get out of bed. My head felt like it had been stomped on, and when there was a knock at my door, it felt like someone was driving a nail through my skull.

"I don't feel well," I called out. The door popped open. Cara stepped inside the room with a bottle of water and closed it behind her. Her face was flawless, even without any makeup, and she was grinning from ear to ear. "How is it you are not suffering as much as I am?" *How can you look so beautiful so effortlessly?*

"I made sure to hydrate throughout the night," she chirped as she held out the bottle and two small aspirin.

"Ugh. I hate you right now." I groaned but took the pills, dropping them into my mouth before guzzling the water.

"Oh, come on. It's not that bad. I'll make you some scrambled eggs, and you'll feel better in no time."

I pulled my quilt over my head, knowing I must look like I just crawled out of a sewer. "Go away, Cara." The image of her mouth pressed against mine played over in my head. *Now that we're both sober, does she regret what happened? Does she even remember?*

The blanket was yanked off, and I curled up, trying to hide my nearly naked body. "Get your lazy little ass up and come downstairs. I'm going to cook eggs, and you're going to tell me what you think of Brody."

"I don't think we can be friends anymore."

Cara rolled her eyes, her hands on her hips, and she groaned loudly. "Too bad you don't have a choice." She wrapped her fingers around my ankle and began to drag me down to the foot of the bed. I clawed desperately at my pillow, hugging it to my chest in hopes it would break my fall when I hit the floor.

"Cara, I'm going to kick you," I called out, but my voice wavered as I struggled not to laugh.

"Bring it," she yelled as she jerked me again and clawed at my blanket.

"What the hell is going on in here?"

Both of our heads snapped to my father, who was standing in my doorway with a look of disapproval.

"I was just trying to get El out of bed," Cara replied, and I had to bite my bottom lip to keep from laughing at how innocent she was trying to appear.

"I'm sure there are more effective methods than assault."

"But none more fun," she shot back with her eyebrow cocked.

"Get downstairs for breakfast. *Now*." My dad shook his head and disappeared down the hall, muttering to himself. As soon as I heard his footsteps began to descend the stairs, I took my pillow and swung, smacking Cara across the face.

"Oh, now I'm going to have to kick your ass," Cara yelled as my father's voice bellowed from the floor below.

"Girls! Come down for breakfast." I was shocked by the anger in his voice.

Cara's shoulders slumped as I rolled out of bed and pulled on my jeans.

"Payback is coming," she threatened, her finger pointed at my nose as I walked around her, sticking out my tongue. Her eyes dropped to my mouth and for a second I was certain she was thinking of our kiss.

I followed her downstairs, unable to wipe the stupid grin from my face, even though my body ached.

Dawn was standing in front of the stove in a fluffy yellow robe, spatula in hand. My dad poured himself a cup of coffee in a plastic to-go cup.

"I'm off." He kissed Dawn on the cheek as she called out for him to drive safely. He nodded to me and Cara as he stalked off toward the front door.

"What's with him?" I asked as I sat down at the table.

"Oh, you know your father," Dawn said before we all fell silent.

"Actually, I don't."

"Oh, honey. I didn't mean…" She turned to face us as she cringed.

"It's fine. It will take some time," I replied, and she seemed to relax. She turned back to the stove, dished scrambled eggs onto our plates, and set them on the table in front of us.

"Thanks." I took a large bite as Dawn made her way to the stairs.

"I have to get ready for work. You girls be good today." Her eyes landed on Cara for an extra minute, and I couldn't suppress my smile. *Why was everyone so concerned with Cara's behavior?*

"What are you laughing at?" Cara asked as I took another bite. "Just eat your dead baby chicken."

I placed my hand over my mouth as my stomach turned. "It's not a dead baby chicken."

"Sure, keep telling yourself that." She grinned as she took a bite. "Peep. Peep."

"Cara…" My stomach rolled again, and I knew if I didn't start thinking of something else, I was going to heave all over the table.

"Oh…that bite was crunchy. Must have been his beak or maybe his little dirty birdy feet."

I felt the bile rise up my throat, and I had to cover my mouth with my hand to keep from launching last night's alcohol all over her, even though it would have served her right. I lurched from the table and ran for the back door, fumbling with the lock before yanking it open. I'd drunk some of my mom's wine before, but hard liquor was something new, and I wasn't sure I'd ever be able to drink it again.

The alarm blasted, causing my head to thump rhythmically. Cara was at my side, gathering my hair and holding it behind me as I heaved my stomach contents off the edge of the deck.

"Jesus, El. I didn't think you'd really throw up. I'm such a bitch. I'm so sorry."

I continued to hurl, completely embarrassed as I tried to wave her away, but she refused to move. I was thankful, since my hair would've been covered in my own vomit had she left. She began to hum, and I rolled my eyes as I dry heaved one last time.

"You…are…a bitch." I groaned as I wiped the back of my hand over my mouth.

"Agreed."

The alarm cut off, and Dawn was now glaring at us, wrapped in a towel with shampoo still slicked in her hair.

"What is going on? Did you not hear the alarm?"

"Sorry, Dawn. El doesn't handle eggs very well, and she didn't want to say anything and hurt your feelings."

Dawn's face softened as a voice called out over the alarm system asking if we needed assistance. She stalked off to speak into the box on the wall as Cara smiled sheepishly at me.

"Forgive me?"

"Never," I growled. I headed back inside with Cara on my heels.

"Why was the alarm set? We never use that thing," Cara asked as she grabbed a bottle of water from the fridge and held it out for me.

"David just thought it would be a good idea. Ellie is new to this town, and he thought it would make her feel safer." Her eyes flashed to me before narrowing on Cara.

Cara's faced hardened. I wondered if this meant that they knew we had snuck out, but neither of them had mentioned it.

"I'm going to go brush my teeth." I hurried up the stairs and into the bathroom. A few minutes later I heard Dawn head into her bedroom, and the sound of water rushing through pipes broke the silence as she continued her shower in the master bathroom.

I scrubbed my tongue with my toothbrush, gagging as the door flew open and Cara stepped inside, her arms crossed over her chest.

"Still mad at me?"

I glanced at her and spit in the sink but didn't respond.

"Still?"

My eyes narrowed as her voice rose another octave.

"How about now?"

I groaned, turning on the water and rinsing my mouth. "No, I'm not mad."

"Good, because I want to do something fun today."

"Oh, God. I don't think I can handle any more of your fun."

"Don't be such a chicken. Sorry. Bad choice of words."

I cupped water from the sink and flung it at her, causing her to scream. "You're not a good person."

"You just figured that out? Get ready. As soon as Dawn leaves we're going out."

"Ugh," I groaned as I looked myself over in the mirror. This was going to be a long day. I ran a brush through my hair as Cara headed off down the hall to her room. I made my way back to my room and looked over my boxes. I didn't have the energy to even change my clothing, but I knew I had to make myself look a little better if I was going to be in public next to Cara.

I grabbed another pair of jean shorts and a navy-blue tank top. Pulling off my bra, I decided not to torture myself by wearing one today. I kicked my panties off and grabbed a clean pair of white boy-shorts.

I shimmied into them and pulled my tank top over my head before slipping into my shorts. As I pulled open my door I jumped, grabbing my chest when Cara was standing right outside with a pair of sunglasses held out in her hand for me. She had another pair propped on top of her head, holding back her hair.

"Thanks."

"It's the least I could do, El." Cara draped her arm over my shoulders as we made our way downstairs and to the front door.

"What about the alarm?"

"I have the code. I'm guessing David just wants to be able to check when it's been turned off so he knows if we left the house. Not a big deal. We're going to the library and will have our books as proof."

"Why doesn't he trust you?" I asked, pulling back from her as I folded my arms.

"Maybe it's *you* he doesn't trust," she countered as she entered the code. I watched her type 4739 into the keypad before averting my gaze so she didn't notice.

"I saw the way he looked at you—like he knows you're up to no good."

Cara pulled open the door and made a sweeping gesture with her arm so I would walk out in front of her. She pulled the door closed behind us before flipping her shades down on her face.

"Well, David has trust issues."

"Mm-hmm."

It was sunny and warm out, perfect for an afternoon stroll, although I half expected to see Tristan parked at the end of the driveway, but the street was practically vacant. Cara pulled her hair from her neck, twisting it into a messy bun and securing it with a hair tie from her wrist. Her large oval sunglasses covered half her face, but you could still tell she was beautiful. No one would have ever guessed she'd spent half the night partying. I, on the other hand, felt like a train wreck, and I was certain my appearance reflected that feeling.

We walked down Main Street for several blocks as my eyes danced over the small storefronts.

"So I figured we can do a little bit of shopping and maybe get lunch while we're out."

"What about the library?" I looked over to Cara who had her chin pointed up toward the sun.

"We'll get you some books, nerd. You already finish that porn?" A smile spread across her face, causing her cheeks to dimple.

"It is *your* book."

"Semantics," she mumbled with a sigh as we walked under a large tree that jutted out of the sidewalk, cloaking her in shade. She stopped abruptly, looking over the glass front of Nifty Thrifty.

"That dress would look killer on you," I said as I looked over the baby-blue knee-length dress on the mannequin.

"Not really my thing." She scrunched up her nose. "But let's see what else they have." She grabbed my hand and pulled me through the door. A bell dinged above our heads as we stepped inside. The air smelled stale, and I had to breathe through my mouth not to spill the contents of my stomach once again.

Cara's fingers slid along the racks of clothing as she walked toward the back of the store, waiting for something to catch her eye. I grabbed a green T-shirt that said "Getting lucky in Kentucky" across the front.

Cara smiled, shaking her head as she let out a small laugh. "I can't picture you wearing something like that."

"Whatever." I hung it back on the rack. "I thought you might like it."

"When I think of someone getting lucky in Kentucky, I'd imagine it was two cousins," she said with a laugh, and the older woman behind the cash register glanced up from behind her glasses, her lips pressed into a thin line.

Cara glanced over at me with a look of embarrassment, and I couldn't help but giggle. *She's adorable.*

"What about these?" She stopped, holding up a pair of silver sparkly heels that were dangerously tall.

"That's a great way of saying 'I charge by the hour,'" I joked, and Cara snorted as she smacked my arm.

"You're not nearly as uptight as you pretend to be, you know that?"

"Thanks…I guess." I took the shoes from her hands and placed them back on the shelf as I shook my head. "Friends don't let friends look like hookers."

Cara pulled her phone from her back pocket as it chimed and read over her message before quickly tapping out a response.

"Tristan and some of the guys are heading over to the Duct Tape Carnival later. You want them to swing by and get us?"

"Duct Tape Carnival? That doesn't sound very fun."

"That's just what the guys call it. They come to town once a year for a few days. The rides are all falling apart and there is duct tape on the seats," she explained with a laugh. "We mostly just go for the games and to eat cotton candy. It will be fun."

"Who all is going?" I turned toward the rack beside me and began thumbing through the clothing. I didn't want her to see my face, because she'd know right away why I was asking.

"He didn't say."

"Hmm…" was all I said as I pulled a yellow dress from the rack and held it up against my body. Cara wrinkled her nose as she shook her head. I slid it back into the rack and ran my fingers through my hair.

"Fine. But if David yells at us, I am placing the blame on you."

"He'd blame me anyway. I won't let him yell at you." Cara beamed as she tapped out a reply to Tristan. We headed back out to the sidewalk with no purchases, but we were far from finished.

CHAPTER TWELVE

Cara

I felt awful for causing El to be sick after I'd kept her out all night, and I wanted to make it up to her. "What is it you want to do?" I looked over at her, her hair blowing slightly in the warm breeze.

"We need to go to the library."

I nodded. "If we must."

"We must. I don't want David to start not trusting me."

"Who cares what he thinks?"

Ellie stopped walking, her hands on her hips. "You do. You sneak around and hide who you are from him."

I swallowed hard as her eyes searched mine. "I don't hide who I am from him." *I hide who I am from everybody.*

Her head cocked to the side, and she smiled coyly. "Of course you do. You're funny and outgoing, and you don't seem to ever let them see that side of you. I think you should."

I smiled back, letting out the breath I'd been holding. "Yeah, I guess I do care what they think." *But maybe I care what you think.*

"Well, we are both guilty of putting on a front to impress others." El began walking, and I followed behind her, letting her know which street to turn down. Her words played over and over in my head. She was right, but it wasn't that simple for me. If I showed the world who I truly was, I'd be ostracized. I could already see the sideways glances toward her from David, and I was worried she would be an outcast soon, too.

"When we are done at the library, I want to go back to Nifty Thrifty so I can prove you wrong," I thought out loud. *I'm willing to try to show the world I don't care.*

After looking over spines of no less than a hundred books, Ellie finally chose one from the romance section titled *The Note*.

"Give up on *The Good Girls*," I teased as we slipped back out into the sunshine. We made our way back to the thrift store, and Ellie questioned me the entire way about what we were going to get. I grabbed the most ridiculous shirt I could find and held it up to Ellie. She scrunched up her nose and giggled at the multicolored monstrosity.

"Okay, did you get high when I wasn't looking?"

"We are not going to care what anyone thinks about us today." I smiled as she looked down over the hideous shirt and nodded with approval.

"Well, we're going to need accessories."

I squealed, and we both began thumbing through the racks for the most horrendous top we could find for each other. Ellie settled on a lime-green halter with layers of sequined ruffles for me. I decided on a crop top that said, "I love wieners," with a picture of a dachshund. When her cheeks turned crimson, I knew it was the perfect choice.

Ellie complemented my green shirt with a floppy pink hat and purple Happy New Year sunglasses. But she was the real winner with pair of cat ears attached to a headband and fanny pack.

We left the store with tears streaming down our cheeks from laughter and grabbed ice cream cones from the Dip.

"You know, I absolutely hate to shop, but today was really fun," El said as she licked her cone of butter pecan.

"It was fun," I replied as I took a bite of my mint chocolate chip. It tasted awful, and I knew I shouldn't have taken the worker's advice that vanilla was boring.

"Is it that bad?" Ellie sighed, taking the cone from my hand and giving me her butter pecan, struggling not to drop our bags. "You're such a baby."

"I like what I like." I shrugged, licking her cone, pleasantly surprised at how good it tasted.

"My mom would only eat chocolate ice cream, and I mean, like, all the time. To this day it...I just can't eat it."

I nodded, glad that she was finally opening up about her mother. I don't even think she meant to. "Too much of a good thing."

"She was always the 'cool mom,' ya know? She let me eat junk food and stay up late on school nights. But we had to work just as hard as we played."

"She sounds really nice." *I wish I could say the same about my mom.*

"She was. I would be so hard on myself if I ever brought home anything less than an A, but my mom would always tell me that it wasn't about the grades you make, but the hands you shake."

"Smart woman. I can see where you get it from."

El smiled as she tucked her hair behind her ears. "She was. She worked really hard for everything we had, so I never wanted to let her down."

"I'm sure you didn't."

She pulled her lip between her teeth as she looked at the ground, obviously debating about whether or not to say something. "The night...it all happened, I felt like I would never be able to laugh again. Nothing would ever be the same." Her eyes met mine for a moment before she smiled. "Thank you. You have no idea how much it means to me that you let me tag along with you."

"Tag along? I like hanging out with you, El. It's helped me a lot, too." *You are the one who is making me feel like myself again.*

"Who is Dawn to you?"

Her question caught me off-guard, and I wasn't sure how much of my past I wanted to divulge. This was supposed to be a new start for me.

"She was a friend of my mother's."

Ellie licked her cone and nodded but didn't press me further, even though I could tell she was curious. "You know what my mother always ate with ice cream? French fries." Her eyes lit up as she looked across the street to Larson's Deli.

"That's really gross." I shook my head as she grabbed my free hand and pulled me across the road. I couldn't wipe the smile from my face, loving this weird and quirky side to her.

CHAPTER THIRTEEN

Ellie

We wandered around Main Street for the next hour, while I ate french fries and Cara gossiped about everyone from school. My head was swimming with all of the useless information that she supplied me with, and I really just wanted to go home and take a nap. But part of me was hoping to see Brody again, and I didn't want to be the girl who couldn't even handle one night of partying.

Tristan met us in the parking lot of Spend and Save, where Cara and I had decided to sit on the curb, our legs stretched out in the sun, our bags of new clothing between us.

"Ladies." Cameron nodded as he glanced out the passenger window at us. My heart sank when I saw the back seat was empty.

We slipped into the back, and Tristan pulled back out on Main Street, turning right down Melvin Avenue.

Cara pulled out my I LOVE WIENERS shirt from her bag and held it out to me.

"What?" I asked as I looked over the shirt.

"We have to change, dummy. We don't want to go to the carnival looking like this."

"We don't?" I asked as I looked toward the guys and noticed Tristan's gaze in the mirror.

"Nope." Cara grabbed the bottom of her tank top and pulled it over her head before slipping her new ruffled, lime-green halter on.

"Cara," I whispered, trying to keep the guys from hearing me. "I'm not changing in the car. I don't have a bra on."

"El, they're just boobs…and both of them have seen women's breasts before," she joked, and both of the guys groaned at her lame joke.

I shook my head, bending down behind the seat so I could pulled my shirt over my head, my body covered in goose bumps. I quickly slid into the ridiculous top feeling like my adrenaline was going to make my heart explode.

"Where are the guys?" Cara asked as I relaxed against the back of the seat next to her. She handed me my cat ears and fanny pack, and I rolled my eyes as I completed my ensemble.

"Luke is working, and I think Brody is still with some chick he met at the party." Tristan's eyes met mine briefly, and I felt my heart sink, the corners of my lips struggling to pull down into a frown.

"Sorry, El." Cara whispered and wrapped her hand around mine. I leaned my head on her shoulder and sighed. It was hard to feel sad when we looked so absolutely silly.

"You can hang out with me today, El. I promise I won't bite," Cameron called over his shoulder, and Cara's shoulders bobbed as she laughed, jarring my head.

"What?" I lifted my head to look at Cara as she struggled to keep her giggles quiet.

"Bingo has a reputation that precedes him," Tristan explained, without really explaining anything at all.

"Vicious rumors," Cameron shot back as he ran his hand over his dark, messy hair, his fingers rubbing the back of his tanned neck.

"Only they're true," Cara chimed in.

"Will someone please tell me what you guys are talking about?" I looked back and forth between them before Tristan cleared his throat.

"Cameron once had an unfortunate incident involving some girl giving him head and a dog thinking that he was being attacked, so the dog bit the girl on the ass."

Cameron groaned. "It wasn't as bad as it sounds, and she bit my dick, so we're even."

"Four stitches in her butt, and she couldn't sit for days. Plus the whole rabies scare." Cara was laughing so hard I could barely make out what she was saying. "They...they...said..."

"They said that she screamed so loud his mom came busting in and passed out from the shock," Tristan finished, his crooked grin reflecting in the rearview mirror.

"I'm sorry I asked," I mumbled, feeling like I stepped into an entirely different world.

"That's not even the best part." Tristan was beaming as he glanced in his mirror at us. "The dog's name was Bing." He started to chuckle, struggling to catch his breath so he could finish. "So he was screaming 'Bing, go! Bing, go!'"

"That actually explains a lot." I laughed, finally understanding his nickname.

I stared out of the side window as we traveled the last several miles to the carnival. My excitement grew as I noticed the large Ferris wheel ahead. I was scared of heights and not a fan of anything fast or seemingly unsafe, but I've always loved to play the little games.

We parked among the endless rows of cars in a large field. I popped open my door and stepped out into the fading sun, looking skyward as I waited for the others to join me.

"Are you really going to force us to be seen in public with the two of you dressed like that?" Tristan shook his head but sighed in resignation as Cara slipped under his arm.

As we began to walk, I shoved both of my hands into my shorts pockets as I trailed behind the three of them.

Cameron was going on and on about the time he wrecked his car and his license was suspended. I didn't realize how far I'd fallen behind them as I let my thoughts wander to my mother. A lump formed in my throat.

When Tristan noticed that I wasn't part of the conversation, he stopped and waited for me to reach his side, his eyebrows pulled together, before putting his other arm around my shoulders. I felt silly, but Cara looked over at me with a smile, and I relaxed.

We walked up to a ticket booth just outside of all of the activity and waited in line.

"I'm going to grab a soda. You guys want anything?" Cameron's eyes landed on me, and I shook my head. He nodded and disappeared through the crowd.

We stepped forward as the line began to move.

"I think he likes you," Cara teased, and I ducked my head.

"Babe, maybe you should give her a few days to get settled before you make her regret coming here." Tristan's arm squeezed me a bit closer to him. "Wasn't having to deal with Brody enough?"

I laughed, but I knew my cheeks were pink as I remembered what dancing with him felt like. "He's not so bad," I replied, tucking my hair behind my ear and glancing up at him. "But we were just having fun." I shrugged. He was right. I didn't want to start anything so soon with anyone. I was just finally having a chance to spread my wings, and I didn't want them clipped.

We stepped up to the man behind the glass sitting in the tiny red-and-white-striped booth.

"Four ticket books," Tristan told him as he unlooped his arms from our shoulders and pulled his wallet from his back pocket.

"I don't have any money." I looked to Cara, embarrassed.

"Don't worry about it. Tristan can afford it." She rolled her eyes as he slipped his wallet back into his pocket and held out a book of tickets for each of us as Cameron reappeared with a soda and a small box of popcorn.

Cara squealed and grabbed my hand, pulling me toward a row of games. "Let's go have some fun."

"Don't go too far. I don't want one of the pervert carnies to get his hands on either of you," Tristan called out, not caring that the man behind the booth could hear him.

"He's so annoying." Cara shook her head as we trailed farther away.

"It's nice he likes to make sure you're safe." I shrugged, even though I found his comment a little more embarrassing than my tacky outfit. But I liked the idea of someone looking after us.

Cara and I played nearly every game we came across but didn't win a single one. As the sun began to set in the sky, we met back up with Tristan and Cameron who were each holding two cups of beer. I took one from Cameron and thanked him as I sipped it down, my eyes roaming over the flashing lights of the rides.

"Shouldn't we be getting back?" I asked, not trying to make myself sound too young in front of the guys, but David was probably home from work by now.

"You're right. We can always sneak back out later." Cara's eyebrow arched, and I rolled my eyes, taking another sip of my beer. "Can we do the haunted house first?"

All eyes turned to me, and I sighed as I let my shoulders sag in defeat. "Fine. But then we need to go." I gave her a warning glare, and she beamed.

"I'll catch up with you guys," Cameron said, clamping his hand down on Tristan's shoulder. My eyes followed his gaze to a group of girls standing by the hot dog stand.

"Beware of the dog," I called out as Cara giggled.

Cara grabbed my hand and pulled me toward the haunted house. It was the walk-through kind with workers dressed in elaborate costumes who jumped out to scare you.

We paid our tickets and slipped inside the darkness. The first room was flashing lights and mirrors everywhere. It took me a full five minutes to figure out the exit. I had to feel the walls to find the next room where I was plunged into darkness as evil laughs echoed in my ears. A clown jumped out in front of me, and I clutched my chest as I let out a squeal, stumbling backward until I collided with someone else.

I jumped as a set of arms snaked around my waist and pulled me against them.

"Get off me!"

"Jesus, El, it's me. It's me." Tristan laughed, his chest rumbling against my back. I struggled to pull from his grip, but his arms tightened around me. I wiggled against him enough to turn around, smacking him across the chest.

"What the hell is wrong with you? I thought I was being attacked."

"You disappeared, so I doubled back to make sure you were okay. Cara is already outside waiting. She was worried."

"I'm fine. I just got lost. Let go of me."

His lip quirked up in a smirk as I tried again to push away from him without success. He was finding my struggling amusing, and it was beginning to really piss me off.

"You're such a baby." His arms unlocked from around me, and I nearly fell backward.

My shoulders slumped as my heart rate finally started to ebb. Tristan slipped his hand in mine and began to pull me through the maze. The next room had creepy-crawly creatures dangling from the ceiling, and I ran into Tristan's back trying to push him through the house faster. As pissed as I was that I was scared, I was glad he'd come back for me.

When we finally reached daylight, I nearly fell onto the grass as I stumbled through the giant spinning cylinder. Cara held out her arms for me, and I released Tristan's hand and ran into her hug.

"That was awful," I grumbled as she pulled back from me, tucking my hair behind my ears.

"You were very brave," he said as he fought against a smile.

I narrowed my eyes and folded my arms over my chest. "Don't patronize me."

"Let's get you guys home so El can change her panties. I'm pretty sure she pissed herself when I found her."

I glared at Tristan, feeling the heat rise in my cheeks from embarrassment. "You scared me on purpose."

"I saved you from the evil clown." He put his hand on his chest, pretending to be hurt.

"I didn't need you to save me. I can take care of myself." I began to walk toward the exit as they followed. *What the fuck is his problem?*

"El, cats have nine lives, you didn't have anything to worry about," Cara called after me, and I pulled the ears from my head.

"A simple thank you is all I—"

I cut him off before he could finish. "Thank you." I held up my middle finger and didn't look back. Cara giggled, and we disappeared through the crowd.

When I reached the car, I waited for Tristan to unlock it. "Where's Cameron?"

"He'll meet up with us later," Tristan answered as he pulled open his door and hit the unlock button for the rest of the doors.

I slid into the backseat, and to my surprise, Cara slid in beside me instead of sitting up front with Tristan.

"I scare guys off fast, it seems."

Tristan laughed as he started the car and pulled out of the parking spot. "It may be your fashion sense."

I glanced down at my silly shirt and laughed. "I'm pretty sure stating that I love wieners should have the opposite effect."

"If it makes you feel any better, I'm pretty sure Cameron loves them, too."

CHAPTER FOURTEEN
Cara

For the first time in as long as I could remember, I truly enjoyed myself. I didn't need to pretend and put on a front. The past meant nothing, and all I could think about was the here and now. But I was always waiting for the other shoe to drop. Trust didn't come easy for someone who's been abandoned and betrayed as many times as I've been.

I put down my window and held my arm out in the warm wind as I relaxed my head against the seat. Ellie lay down with her head in my lap. I stroked her hair, and she fell asleep before we even made it home.

I woke her up as we pulled up to the end of our long driveway. She stretched with a loud yawn before we got out and slowly made our way down the driveway with her library book in hand.

When we opened the front door, Dawn was in the kitchen, and her attention turned to us.

"Where have you two been?" she asked as she washed a plate and set it in the dish rack.

"We went to the library," Cara said. Dawn put her hands on her hips, glaring at us.

We both burst out laughing when we realized we'd forgotten to change out of our outfits.

"Oh…we stopped at that little thrift shop in town. We were just having some fun," I said as we walked into the kitchen and grabbed two plates from the cupboard.

"Well, you should change before David finishes his shower," she warned us, and I rolled my eyes as I dished spaghetti onto each of our plates.

We both ran up the stairs and changed out of our silly clothes before returning to the table to eat, only a minute before David's heavy footsteps descended the stairs.

"Ellie, I wondered where you'd gotten to," he said with faked enthusiasm that seemed to be more for Dawn's benefit. *Don't worry about me. I'm safe, too.*

"I went to the library with Cara, and we checked out a few of the stores," she said as she neatly cut up the strands of pasta before twirling her fork against her spoon. This couldn't be the same girl who was dipping fries in her ice cream cone and walking around all day wearing a shirt that proclaimed she loved wieners.

I giggled, and David's glare cut to me. "Something funny?"

I cleared my throat as I spun my fork in my noodles. "I was just thinking of how gross it was that Ellie ate french fries with her ice cream." I wrinkled my nose as I saw her trying not to smile.

"Just like your mother. She always was weird," he said. He cleared his throat like he hadn't intended to speak aloud.

Her smile faltered as she looked down at her plate, and I knew she was struggling to suppress her tears. *We had such a great day. Way to fucking ruin it, David.*

"I thought it was unique."

She glanced up at me, and the corners of her mouth turned up.

"Well, you don't exactly conform to society's standard of normal, do you?" He muttered as he pulled open the fridge behind me. "What the hell would you know?"

"David!" Dawn scolded him.

"I'll be in my office if anyone needs me," he said as he cracked open a soda and disappeared down the short hall behind the kitchen.

"I think I lost my appetite." I shoved my chair back causing it to screech loudly across the wooden floor before I dropped my fork on my plate and stormed up the stairs. I'd finally found someone who liked me for who I really was, even if she didn't know the whole story, and David was going to take that away from me.

I took the stairs two at a time and slammed my bedroom door behind me when I was safely inside.

CHAPTER FIFTEEN
Ellie

I looked to Dawn, who was still standing by the sink, her mouth agape as she tried to process what had just happened. I picked up my napkin and wiped my mouth before I stood, leaving my plate on the table as Cara had, and hurried upstairs.

I froze with my hand just inches from her wooden door as I heard her muffled sobs coming from the other side. I took a deep breath and knocked before turning the knob and slipping inside, closing it behind me.

Cara sat on her bed, her knees pulled to her chest. Her cheeks were stained with tears. She was far from the confident, outgoing girl I'd seen.

I sank down beside her on the mattress and wrapped my arms around her. She released her hold on her legs and wrapped her arms around my body, pulling me tightly against her as she wept.

"It's okay," I whispered as she shook her head against the crook of my neck.

"No. He's right."

"Cara, don't say that. He just doesn't know you."

"He doesn't *want* to know me, Ellie."

I pulled back from her slightly and put my hands on either side of her face as I looked into her shimmering green eyes that glowed against the redness from her tears. "*I* want to know you." My eyes searched hers as her lips parted and a small sigh escaped her.

Her soft lips pressed against mine, unmoving. My fingers slid into her hair, tangling in the long strands as I held her against me. I had no idea what I was doing. The first time we kissed I told myself we'd had too much to drink. Now I had no idea why she'd done it. Her lips parted, and she ran the tip of her tongue over my lower lip. I felt it through every inch of my body. I let my lips part, allowing her access.

Cara's tongue swept against mine before she pulled my lower lip between hers, sucking it gently before we broke apart. Her forehead rested against mine, and she kept her eyes closed as she struggled to calm her breathing.

"I'm so sorry, El." She shook her head, her eyebrows pulled together like she was in pain.

"It's okay," I reached for her but she stood, backing herself up against her wall next to her bed with her arms wrapped around her waist.

I pushed from the bed and took a step toward her, but she pressed herself farther into the wall as if hoping to disappear. Guilt consumed me. She was disgusted by what we'd done, and even though I was confused, regret was the last thing I felt.

Humiliation began to creep into my subconscious as Cara refused to meet my eye. I pulled open her door and slipped into the hallway, begging myself not to break down until I reached my room.

When I did, the emotions flooded me like a broken dam. It was all too much to take in. Cara was being kind to me, and she was the only person I had. That's all this was, and now she was sickened by me. I had no idea how I'd be able to fix this, but I had to do something.

I lay on my bed for hours, my face buried in my pillow before the doorknob creaked and Cara slipped inside of my room. I had to force myself to look up at her. She smiled weakly as she wrung her hands together.

"Are you still mad at me?" she asked as she tucked her hair behind her ear.

"I was never mad at you, Cara." I turned on my side to face her. "I thought…" I struggled to express what I was thinking, but I was so confused; I had no idea what to say.

"I don't want to be alone," she said quietly, her gaze dropping to the floor. I patted the empty space beside me on the bed.

Cara walked toward my bed and pulled up the quilt before slipping underneath and draping her arm across my waist. Her face was only a few inches from mine. I could barely make out her features in the dark, but the mint of her breath washed over my face rhythmically as she hummed the same haunting melody she had so many times before. Soon it evened out, and I drifted off to sleep beside her.

I awoke a few hours later, burning up. My legs were tangled in Cara's, and my arm was slung over her small stomach, our foreheads pressed together.

I pulled back slightly, preparing to roll over as her arms tightened around me. I glanced over her shoulder to my alarm clock on the table beside my bed. It was nearly four o'clock in the morning.

"Cara," I whispered, and she groaned, pulling my hips against hers, rolling back slightly so I was half on top of her. "Cara." I slid my hand over her cheek as her eyes fluttered open. She looked confused before recognition washed over her and her expression softened.

"You have to go back to your room before David and Dawn get up."

With a sleepy smile, she stretched her body underneath me before I slid to my side and let her up so she could leave.

CHAPTER SIXTEEN
Cara

Long summer days never seemed to last, and soon the weeks blurred by as if it had been one big long kegger. Ellie and I never spoke about the times we'd kissed or about the many nights I'd slipped into her room so I didn't have to sleep alone. I loved having her close. She was the only person who looked me in the eye and saw past my bullshit.

I dreaded having to go back to school, and I wanted to make the most of the time we had left. I'd been trying to figure out a way to break it to Tristan that I was going to be a senior and I wouldn't be joining him in college, but he'd been growing more withdrawn after his parents told him they would be getting a divorce.

Tonight we were on a personal mission to make Tristan have fun, and El and I were going to pull out all the stops. I called up Brody and the other guys and told them to meet us at the local swimming hole for a barbecue.

I didn't have a grill to drag out there, so instead I picked up burgers and fries from Larson's Deli and a milkshake for El, because ketchup wouldn't work for her fries like a normal person. *I love that about her.*

She tried to pretend to be offended when I gave it to her, but I knew she was happy that I'd remembered. And she drank the entire thing before Tristan even came for us.

Tristan picked us up outside of the restaurant, and I gave him directions to the local swimming hole where we were met by the other guys.

"Why didn't you tell me this was where we were going, babe? What's all this about?" Tristan looped his arm around my neck and pulled me into his side as he placed a kiss on top of my head.

"You said when you were little you loved to go camping and have cookouts with your mom and dad. This was the best I could do. I wanted to see you smile for a change." I shrugged as he took the bags of food from me and kissed me on the lips.

"You're fucking amazing, you know that?"

"Of course I know that," I joked as Brody ran over and lifted Ellie over his shoulder, causing her to scream. This was quickly becoming their thing. He would pick her up and scare the hell out of her—any excuse to touch her. She would pretend to be offended, but I knew she liked that he was so playful. It shouldn't have bothered me, but it did, and I noticed myself slowly taking on Tristan's dislike of him.

He finally set her down gently at the edge of the water, and she smacked him on his bare chest, but the blush in her cheeks let me know she enjoyed it.

"Babe, where are all the fries? There's like half a container in here." Tristan held up the cardboard box with a confused frown.

"That would be El's fault." I took it from him and pulled out a fry, shoving it in my mouth.

"You didn't want to see me smile, El?" he teased as he looked over at Ellie, who was peeling off her T-shirt and shorts to reveal a baby-blue bikini I'd lent her. Brody's eyes were fixed on her body, and he didn't even pretend that he wasn't gawking. She shrugged, causing the other guys to laugh. "Send her overboard, Bro." Brody ran for Ellie, grabbing her around the waist as they both fell into the murky water with loud screams.

As they broke the surface, Ellie was cursing Brody, trying to smack him and cling to him for dear life at the same time. I laughed, loving how her prim and proper vernacular was now more suited for a sailor.

"Don't let her drown," I called out, shaking my head with my hands on my hips.

"She'll be fine." Tristan held out a burger for me, and I took it as I rolled my eyes. "I'll kick his ass if he hurts her."

"Oh, sure. *Now* you trust Brody." I sank down on a fallen tree trunk and unwrapped my food as Tristan settled next to me on the log.

"I just know he likes to play with a lot of girls, but El's different. She's one of us now. None of us would let anything happen to her or you."

Cameron walked over and grabbed a burger, sitting down on the other side of me as we ate and looked out over the water.

"Where the fuck are the fries?" he asked. Tristan chuckled as I let out a frustrated groan.

"Again, El, with the fries?" Cameron yelled. "That's coldhearted, woman."

"I got it," Brody shouted as he pushed Ellie's head under the water.

Her arms flailed as she came back to the surface.

"I'm going for a swim. You coming?" I pulled off my shirt and slid my shorts down my thighs before adjusting my white bikini. Cameron's eyes traveled up my legs and over my chest before Tristan punched him in the arm.

"What the fuck, Bingo?" Tristan growled, his temper now being triggered much faster by everything going on in his family. I sighed as I walked closer to him, straddling his legs so his eyes were level with my chest.

"I'm going to go get wet." I bent down and kissed him, feeling him relax under my touch.

"Let me make you wet." He winked as he reached around my waist.

Pulling back from his hold, I ran and jumped into the water, splashing Brody and El as they both cursed me. Seconds later Luke swung in on the old knotted rope that hung on a tree on the other side of the creek, splashing the rest of us.

Tristan didn't take long to join us as the guys began to talk about playing chicken. He sank below the surface of the water and lifted me onto his shoulders as Brody did the same with El, his fingers sliding up her thighs.

"I don't know what to do." El giggled as Tristan stepped closer to them. I reached for her hands. Sliding my fingers in hers.

"We are just going to try to push each other down," I explained as the guys began to talk trash from under us, although I was sure neither was eager to have us off them.

We began to fight as the guys stumbled back and forth, struggling to outlast the other. I was so wrapped up the fun of it all that I didn't notice Luke coming up from behind Brody until the knot on El's bikini string sprang free. She struggled to unhook our hands and grasp at her top, bending over to shield her chest and throwing Brody off-balance. They fell forward fast, not giving Tristan enough time to move us out of her path. Our heads collided with a thud before both guys sank under the water, submerging us in the process.

I swam to the surface, gasping for air as I spun around, looking for Ellie. Tristan stood and then Ellie, causing me to sigh in relief as she stayed ducked low to retie her string. I looked around for Brody, calling his name but he'd yet to come up. All of a sudden, El screamed, her arms flailing as she disappeared under the water, and Brody popped up, laughing as she stumbled, trying to catch her footing in the silt.

I smacked Luke's arm hard, causing it to crack loudly from the wetness.

"Jesus Christ, Cara. What was that for?" he barked, and Tristan stepped in front of me like he needed to defend my honor.

"You could have drowned Ellie, and you made us bang fucking heads."

"But he didn't." El stepped between the two guys with a bright, playful smile on her face. "It's fine. I'm all right."

"No, it's not fucking fine. You think exposing her tits to all of us here is some kind of fucking joke?" Tristan reached around Ellie and shoved Luke. Brody was at Tristan's side, shoving him hard, causing him to slam into me in the process.

"Don't touch my fucking brother, Tris." Brody's voice was frighteningly deep, and the situation was quickly getting out of hand.

Ellie reached for me when she saw me get knocked sideways. Tristan stood tall, pushing his chest against Brody's, and I knew this was going to end horribly. I reached for Tristan's arm, which swung back to shake off whoever had ahold of him, causing his elbow to collide with my cheekbone. I screamed as the pain radiated throughout my face. Ellie grabbed me, pulling me against her chest as she stroked my wet hair, and the guys went nuts.

"Fuck, Cara. What the hell were you doing?" He pulled me from Ellie's grip as she reluctantly released her hold on me. He pulled me into him, crushing me against his muscular body. "Look what the fuck you made me do," he called over his shoulder to Brody who threw his hands in the air.

"Get her out of the fucking water so we can make sure she's okay," Brody yelled, but the anger had left him, and he was now concerned about me.

Tristan shook his head but turned and climbed up the bank, pulling me behind him as I held my throbbing face.

After assuring everyone that I was all right and agreeing that it was stupid to stand behind two men fighting, the commotion died down. Ellie wouldn't stop staring at me with a sympathetic pout.

The pain began to fade after a few drinks, and the guys made sure I always had something in my hand.

We drank beer for hours, and as the sun began to set, the guys gathered old pieces of broken up wood and started a small bonfire. We sat on our towels around the flickering flames and told embarrassing stories. El had been quietly listening to everyone as she watched the fire.

"What about you, El? Any embarrassing stories to share with the group?" I cocked an eyebrow as she looked down at the ground.

"Um…one time I vomited my breakfast in front of someone," she replied dryly, and I couldn't help but laugh.

"You were having breakfast together. We know what that means," Luke called out, and the guys all laughed. I wanted to stand up for her and tell them she wasn't a whore, but I knew it would sound weird coming from me, and she seemed to laugh it off.

"Someone you liked?" Brody sat forward, wanting to know more about Ellie as well. He was like a dog being teased by a bone when it came to her. She had yet to kiss him, and I knew the thrill of the chase was driving him crazy. But I was worried that once he got what he wanted from her, he'd break her heart.

El's eyes flicked to mine before she tossed a small twig on the fire. "Yeah." The corners of her mouth twitched, but she didn't look my way again.

"We should get you guys back." Tristan stood, stretching his tanned, muscular body before holding out his hand to help me from the ground.

"Are you coming back for us later?" I asked as he pulled me against his chest, his fingers on the bare flesh of the small of my back.

"Maybe," he teased as he kissed me.

"Maybe?"

"I was hoping we could spend some time alone tonight." He pulled my hips tight against his so I would know exactly what he wanted to do.

"But there's the party over at Brasher's." I stuck out my lower lip, and he grazed over it with his teeth.

"Fine, but you owe me."

"Yeah, yeah." I looped my arms around his neck and pulled his mouth back against mine, kissing him deeply.

When we got back home, David had pulled me aside to question where Ellie and I had been as she disappeared upstairs to shower. "Getting in later and later." His eyes settled on my swollen pink cheek.

I groaned as I turned to face him. "We were just out swimming with some friends."

"Guys?"

"Would it make you happier if I said I took your daughter around a bunch of horny guys, David? Or would you prefer it was just her and me?"

He cleared his throat, and I knew I'd made him uncomfortable. David knew why I was here, and he did not agree with how my mother treated me, but that didn't mean he was accepting of the things I'd done. In fact, it was more than obvious I was only here so he could earn points with Dawn. That's why I made it a point to hug his precious little girl in front of him the moment I met her. He hadn't stopped glaring at me since.

"Ellie has been through a lot, and she doesn't need to be spending so much time with someone who doesn't have her best interests at heart."

"How do you know what she's been through, David?" I couldn't help but get defensive when it was my shoulder Ellie had been crying on, and her father barely spoke five words to her in a day. "Have you spoken to her? Do you even care how she has been dealing with the death of her mother, the only *real* parent she's ever had?"

"Watch how you talk to me, Cara. You're eighteen in only a week."

"What is that supposed to mean?" I felt my heart sink as I thought of where I would go if David kicked me out. "You going to take away the only person your daughter has who cares about her? She'd never forgive you after that." *Please don't take her away from me.*

"It means that if I think your friendship with my daughter is detrimental to her, I'll have to do what is right for her."

"Like abandon her? Or am I the one who will get left behind this time? It's really hard to tell who you care about less." I folded my arms over my chest, begging my lower lip to stop quivering. There is no way Dawn would let him just kick me out. She couldn't.

He leaned in closer to me, his finger pointed at my face. "You have one week. I suggest you make things right with your mother…and God."

He turned and walked away as I grabbed the banister, sinking down on the bottom step. The tears poured from me as I struggled to think about what I was going to do. Maybe Tristan would let me stay at his apartment with him. I was sure his roommates wouldn't mind having a girl around, and I could get a job. No one actually expected me to graduate high school anyway.

"Cara?" Ellie called from upstairs, and I wiped my cheeks quickly and cleared my throat.

"I'll be right up."

"Shower's free," she replied as I heard her bedroom door close.

I would have to figure all of this out tomorrow. I didn't want El to know what was happening before I knew what I was going to do. For all I knew, David hadn't even talked to Dawn. There was no way she'd let him kick me out with nowhere to go.

I hurried upstairs and slipped into the bathroom, ignoring my pink, tearstained face as I undressed and slid under the hot water.

I hated the idea of leaving Ellie here alone. I knew the guys would look out for her, but I was worried just how much I could trust Brody with her heart.

I hurried through my shower and got dressed quickly before El knocked on my door.

"Come in," I called out as I put mascara on my lashes and covered my lips with gloss.

"You look great," Ellie said approvingly as she looked me over.

"It's just an old pair of jeans," I shook my head as I ran my fingers through my hair.

"Everything okay?" she asked as she stepped closer.

"I'm fine." *Please let it go.*

She grabbed my shoulder and turned me to face her. "You're lying." Her eyes searched mine, and I had to look at the floor to keep from breaking down again.

"Ellie, I'm fine. I promise." I smiled, and she nodded slightly, dropping the subject.

We both slipped downstairs into the living room, and I handed Ellie the remote, letting her flip the channels as my mind wandered off. It wasn't long before the lights in the house were being turned off, and Dawn and David said good night and headed up to bed.

We slipped out of the front door and ran down the driveway, laughing the entire way before diving into Tristan's car. If I only had a few days left with El, I was going to make the best of it. I would worry about calling my mother tomorrow.

CHAPTER SEVENTEEN
Ellie

My blood felt as if it was pulsing through my body to the beat of the song thumping in the background. I looped my arms around Cara's neck as her hands slid down my sides, resting on my hips as our bodies ground together on the dance floor.

We danced like this all the time now, and no one really batted an eye, although many loved to watch us.

"I think you've had a little too much," I whispered.

Cara's eyes were unfocused, and there was some lingering anger under the surface, but she wouldn't tell me what was wrong. *Why won't you trust me?*

"What are you, my mom now?" Cara slurred, and my heart sank at how cold she was being. I knew she hated her mother, and the comparison was meant as an insult. I tried to pull away from her, upset that she wouldn't open up to me, but she grabbed my hands and pulled me back to her.

"I'm sorry, El. Dance with me, please."

She pulled me flush against her body as she began to move her hips again.

"Come on. I don't want you to be upset with me. You can't be upset with me. Not this week."

"Why not this week, Cara?" I asked as I began to dance with her.

"Not any week, Ellie Belly," she replied playfully, and I couldn't help but smile and shake my head.

"I don't understand you," I murmured as a new song began to play. Everyone began to yell, excited for their song to come on.

"You're the *only* one who understands me."

I pressed my forehead against hers and closed my eyes as I let my mind get lost in the lyrics of the song. It was torture not to lean in and kiss her. I wanted to comfort her, take her mind off whatever it was that was plaguing her.

She threw her head back and laughed as Tristan came up behind her and began to dance against her back. The air was thick, and our exposed skin was slick with sweat, but that wouldn't stop the party. My leg was between Cara's, and hers between mine as our hips ground together. Tristan had his face above Cara's shoulder, looking down between us as he watched us move. He took my hand from her neck and slipped it around his. I could feel his pulse thumping beneath my fingertips.

"You two look fucking hot right now," he whispered into her ear, but his eyes were locked on mine.

"It takes no effort for Cara," I replied, and he smirked, clearly oblivious that something was going on with her.

He then reached forward, placing his hands over Cara's on my hips and pulling me tighter against her.

A few guys in the crowd cheered, and our hips swayed wilder with every howl of encouragement. Our chests were pressed together, and I could feel her nipples harden against mine, even in the sweltering heat.

"I thought you didn't like the idea of two girls together," I mumbled, the liquor making the words pour out without thinking. *If you only knew how many nights we spent tangled together like this.*

"I don't mind if I'm with them." He smirked, and I rolled my eyes.

"Let's give them a show," Cara whispered mischievously before pressing her mouth to mine. I was shocked at her sudden public display of affection, but I didn't hesitate in parting my lips. The partygoers roared in approval, but the sound of my heart beat thudding in my ear muffled the sound. I could feel Tristan's hot breath against my cheek, his face dangerously close to ours.

He pressed his mouth to Cara's cheek, and she turned her head to kiss him as I dug my teeth into my lower lip, my body still moving against her to the beat of the music as I watched them make out only an inch from me.

"Kiss, El," she whispered, and before I could protest, Tristan's lips were on mine. He didn't even hesitate. His touch was harder, more forceful than Cara's, but I melted against his mouth. A deep rumble resonated from the back of his throat, and my knees nearly buckled. As he pulled back from me, I stared into his pale-blue eyes, transfixed by how he was looking at me with such want. My eyes went to Cara's, not believing that she was okay with what was happening.

We danced through that song and the next as if it were perfectly normal that the three of us were so close.

"Follow me," Cara whispered into my ear before her teeth grazed my earlobe, sending a shiver down my spine. I smiled, and Tristan ran his tongue over his lower lip as he grabbed Cara's hand and pulled her toward the hallway. My fingers laced in her free hand as I trailed behind them, not allowing myself to second-guess what I was doing.

We slipped into a bedroom, and I pushed the door closed. Leaning back against it, I watched as Tristan pulled Cara against his chest, kissing her hard as she whimpered. I felt uncomfortable, like I was seeing something I shouldn't be, something I knew she had done with him, but it was different to witness it. My thoughts became irrational as I grew angrier, accusing him in my head of taking advantage of her after she'd been drinking, even though I knew Cara well enough to know she was perfectly in control. My fingers gripped the doorknob behind me just as they broke free from each other, and Cara reached for me.

She took my hand and tugged me toward her as Tristan pulled his shirt over his head, his muscles flexing as his hand ran down over his stomach muscles.

"What are we doing?" I asked as her hands gripped my sides.

"Just having some fun." Cara pressed her mouth against mine, her tongue moving over mine as it had so many times when we were alone. Her fingers slipped under my shirt and her palm pressed against my breast.

As Tristan came up behind me and pressed against my back, I broke free from our kiss as I felt how turned on he was by us.

"I…I can't do this." I stepped out from between them and tugged down my shirt, feeling like a fool, fighting against the fog of alcohol in my brain. "*Why* are you doing this?" My eyes searched Cara's, and the sadness I'd seen earlier was back, but she didn't say anything. "I need to go home." I hurried to the door and left before either of them could protest.

CHAPTER EIGHTEEN

Cara

"**S**hit. I have to go after her."

Tristan stepped in front of the door with his hands in front of him. "Babe, you can't just leave."

"I have to, Tristan. She doesn't have a ride home, and I'm not even sure she knows which direction home is."

"So what the fuck am I supposed to do after you and your little cocktease pull this shit?"

My eyes narrowed as my anger sobered me up. "You can go fuck *yourself*."

He pushed off the door, towering over me as he glared down into my eyes. "What the fuck did you say?"

My heart felt like it was beating hard enough to crack my ribs. Tristan had always been intense, but this was the first time I was legitimately scared for my safety.

"I just need to find El. I can't let her out there with all of those guys." I kept my voice even and struggled to keep from looking intimidated. Tristan stepped to the side and waved his arm, granting me permission to leave.

I shouldered by him and out the door as I walked through the crowded house in search of Ellie. I hoped she hadn't really tried to go home on her own.

I made my way down the narrow hall and into the dining room as the music seemed to pulse with my mind. Cameron was talking to some girl as his hand slid over her hip, and I struggled to focus my eyes to appear coherent.

"Cam, have you seen El?" My words slurred, and I didn't even sound like myself.

He glanced around before he shook his head. "Last I saw she was being dragged away by you and Tristan. He didn't last very long, huh?" He smiled as he ran his tongue over his lower lip. *What the fuck have I done?*

"You know where Brody is?" I struggled to choke back the bile that was rising in my throat. I'd managed to destroy El's reputation before I was going to leave her. Fucking perfect.

"After he watched what I saw, he left with some girl from Eastern. You know he had a thing for El. That shit was cold, Cara. Not that I blame you."

"Fuck." I squinted through the fog of alcohol in my head and the fog of smoke in the house and continued on, trying to find her. I couldn't worry about Brody's feelings right now.

After searching all of the unlocked rooms and the bathroom twice, I made my way out front so I could look up and down the road. Just as I turned back toward the house with my head hanging, I heard her voice.

"I don't understand you."

My head snapped up, and I looked off to the left of the house, my eyes struggling to adjust to the darkness. She stepped forward and was now in the glow of the porch light. *You look like an angel.*

"You fucking scared me, El." I stumbled toward her, and she stopped.

"What is going on with you? Something is obviously bothering you, and you won't talk to me, and then you try to get me to fuck your boyfriend?"

"I was there," I mumbled as I squeezed my eyes closed, trying to make my head stop spinning.

"I'm aware. I was aware as I watched you making out with him in front of me. Is that how you think I wanted to lose my fucking virginity, with some guy who is dating my best friend?"

My heart cracked and splintered in my chest. "I just thought…" my voice trailed off as I tried to form a coherent response without telling her the truth. I knew trying to get them together was a stupid move, but at least he'd watch after her if I couldn't. *God, I've had way too much to drink.*

"You *didn't* think. You *didn't* think about my feelings at all." She turned around as she huffed, her hands twisting. *Please don't hate me. You can't hate me. I can't leave you knowing you hate me.*

"Please don't turn away from me." I stepped toward her and put my hand on her shoulder. She turned around slowly, tears streaking down her cheeks, and my heart stuttered. "I'm so fucking sorry, Elise." I pulled her against me, and she reluctantly wrapped her arms around my neck as I rubbed my hands over her back. "I have no idea what I was thinking. I shouldn't have ever put you in that situation."

"I just don't understand you." She sighed against my neck, causing me to shiver and pull her tighter against my body.

She pulled back from me, and I used the pads of my thumbs to wipe away the tears on her cheeks. "Please don't hate me."

"I could never hate you, Cara. Don't you know that by now?" I knew what she meant by what she didn't say. It made me physically ache to be closer to her, even when her body was pressed against mine. I glanced around us, nervous someone might see us embracing, but the only other people outside were more concerned with vomiting or making out. I began to walk forward with Ellie in my arms until we were cloaked in shadows.

"I should never have put you in that situation, El. You mean too much to me."

She pressed her forehead against mine as she nodded slightly. I let my eyes fall closed, relishing her embrace, knowing I wouldn't get to do this much longer.

"You kissed me in front of everyone," she whispered so quietly only I could hear her. I smiled as I tilted my chin up so our lips were nearly brushing.

"I couldn't help myself," I confessed as her lips spread into a smile. I raised my hand and brushed my fingers over the apple of her cheek and down her jaw before her mouth pressed against mine. She mumbled something against my lips but I couldn't make out her words as we deepened our kiss. My hand slid around the back of her neck, holding her close to me, afraid she might disappear if I didn't cling to her. She was like gravity, and my head was constantly in the clouds. I needed her to keep me grounded.

As she pulled away, her eyes searched mine. There was so much left unsaid, but I knew it would be wrong of me to tell her everything I was feeling when I would be out of her life in a matter of days. My entire body felt like it was slowly burning from the inside out. I forced a smile, pretending the pain wasn't consuming me.

"Do you want to go back inside?"

El nodded as she slipped her hand in mine. I pulled her toward the porch. "I just want to go use the bathroom quickly. I'll find you."

I reluctantly let go of her hand and wandered off to find Tristan. I'd felt my phone vibrating in my pocket as I talked to El, but I didn't want to answer it until I knew she was okay. I hoped he wasn't too pissed. I felt so much guilt as it was for what I was doing to El. It was too much to even allow myself to think about how I'd been hurting him, too.

CHAPTER NINETEEN

Ellie

As I rounded the corner, I stopped short when I heard Tristan's voice. His tone was calm, but it was his words that frightened me. "Where the fuck were you?"

"Tristan, I told you I was looking for El."

"You blew me off. I don't fucking appreciate it."

"That hurts," she whimpered.

I stepped into view and cleared my throat, causing Cara to jump, her hand on her chest. Tristan took a step back from her as his arm fell to his side. I watched her fingers slide over her forearm, and I knew he'd done something to hurt her. There'd been many times I'd witnessed his temper, and Cara had bruises that she'd try to explain away. I had no reason not to believe her, and Tristan was always kind and protective of me. As the pieces clicked into place, my stomach sank. Had he been hurting her all this time, and I never knew?

"Damn, El. You scared me." Cara laughed nervously.

My gaze went to Tristan and back to Cara. I could see the embarrassment in her eyes. "Sorry. I…uh…just wanted to thank you for hanging out with me earlier. I really needed that talk about my mom. It helped. So... thanks." I smiled, my eyes dancing between them. Cara's shoulders slumped with relief, and Tristan's features softened, the furrow in his brow smoothing.

"Anytime," Cara replied as she looked to Tristan.

"I'm glad she was there for you." His eyes fell to Cara. "Maybe next time just send me a text, okay, babe? I had no idea where you'd gone. You know how that bothers me." He pressed his lips to her forehead before his gaze flicked to me, and he stalked out of the room.

"What was that about?" I asked as I stepped closer to her.

"I blew him off to go look for you. I should have texted him." Her eyes did not meet mine.

"He sounded really angry."

"He's just been having a hard time with his parents, and they keep dragging him into all of their fights. Plus, I think he was kind of pissed when I left him with blue balls."

I looped my arms around Cara's shoulders and pulled her to my side. "Can you take me home, please?"

Cara nodded, laying her head on my shoulder as we went to find the guys.

The trip home was excruciatingly quiet, and I welcomed the bowl as it was passed back to me, more than happy to let a high wash away the stress of the evening. Cara sat up front next to Tristan, and I sat in the back, sandwiched between Luke and Cameron. Every few minutes Tristan's eyes would land on mine in the mirror, and I knew he was still upset over what had happened earlier. I averted my gaze and tried to pretend nothing had happened.

By the time we made it home, I was practically shoving Cameron out of the door so I could get out of the stifling car and take a deep breath. We slipped into the house without making a sound, and I was surprised that when I went into my bedroom, Cara slipped in behind me and closed the door.

"What are you doing?" I asked as I slid my jeans down my legs and kicked them off onto the floor.

"I really am sorry about earlier."

I shrugged as I pulled down my quilt and slid into bed. "It's fine. I just wish you would tell me what is going on with you. Tonight was so out of character for you." *What are you keeping from me?*

"You don't even know me." She laughed sardonically as she shook her head.

"I don't *know* you? I knew that something has been bothering you all evening, and your own fucking boy-friend couldn't even tell."

"That's not fair."

"No, what's not fair is the position you put me in with your selectively homophobic significant other. What if he had gotten pissed off? Did you even think of that?"

"I wasn't thinking at all, okay?" Her voice rose, and she snapped her mouth shut, trying to curb her anger. "We talked about this. I thought we were okay."

"I don't like the way he was talking to you when I found you guys." I rolled to my side as I watched her pace the floor.

"It doesn't even matter."

"It matters to *me*, Cara, because *you* matter to me."

She stopped pacing and looked over to me. "Tristan and I won't be seeing each other much longer."

"Why is that?" I sat up, shocked and ashamed to say I was hopeful. Was she going to break up with him? *Are you choosing me?*

Shaking her head she looked over me. "School starts soon, and once he finds out I'm still actually in high school, he will end things anyway."

"Oh," I wasn't sure why her answer bothered me, but I was happy that I wouldn't have to worry about her being with someone who wasn't treating her right. I patted the bed beside me and she smiled as she slipped her jeans down over her hips, leaving her in nothing but a gray tank top and black panties.

Turning off the light, she crawled into bed beside me, causing the mattress to dip beside me as I rolled onto my back.

"I'm still mad at you," I whispered, and she slid her hand over my stomach and cuddled against my side, pulling her body tight against me.

"I know, Ellie. I'm sorry I fucked up." Her thumb brushed back and forth over the exposed flesh below my shirt causing goose bumps to spread under her touch.

Sighing loudly, I let my hand rest on hers to stop her from distracting me. "I know."

After a few minutes the silence between us began to eat away at me. I hated holding grudges against Cara. She was my one true friend, and I knew she was battling something internally.

"Is it weird that I'm a virgin?" I whispered as I let out a small giggle, my high still going strong.

"Kind of. Is it weird that I'm not?" I couldn't see her face, but I could hear the smile in her voice.

"Kind of," I replied as her fingers tickled my ribs, causing me to jump.

"It's not that big a deal. I mean, once it's over, you realize it really isn't as exciting as everyone says."

"Really? Tristan is so…"

"What?"

I shrugged, even though we were shrouded in darkness. "You know. Aggressive and masculine."

"Oh really? I guess he is. It's just…I dunno. It's just kind of…boring."

We both laughed, and I had to hold my hand over my mouth to keep myself quiet.

"It's true. I have more fun on my own."

"Oh my God, are you talking about…" I let my voice trail off, too embarrassed to even say the words.

The bed shifted as Cara pushed herself up on her elbow and I could feel her warm breath fan over my face. "Holy shit, El. Please tell me you've at least done *that*."

I bit down on my lower lip and squeezed my eyes closed.

"El, are you serious?"

"Yes, Cara," I snapped, but I couldn't help but laugh.

"You know, I can tell when you're lying, even when I can't see your face."

I laughed, but when Cara was silent, my giggle died in my throat. Her face was closer now, our breath mingling as my body hummed with anticipation. With all of my doubts earlier, I knew exactly what I wanted right now, and I wanted Cara more than anything.

"Maybe I have," I whispered.

"What do you think about when you touch yourself, El?" She spoke so quietly that I was certain she could hear my heart as it began to hammer inside of my chest.

"What do *you* think about?"

"You," she whispered against my lips. Her fingers slid over my cheek as she inhaled before her mouth moved against mine. I tangled my fingers in her hair as my tongue dragged against her lower lip. She sighed as her mouth opened, her tongue eagerly moving against mine. Our pants sounded deafeningly loud in the quiet space.

Rolling onto her back, she pulled me on top of her, her hands sliding down my back and over my ass as she pulled me closer. I rocked my hips, gasping into her mouth at the feel of her body against mine. She dragged her hands higher, pushing my shirt up my body, until her thumb slid over my nipple, which hardened under her touch.

I pressed against her touch as our kiss deepened, wanting more but not certain what it was I wanted her to do. I couldn't get enough of her. I needed her everywhere.

She slipped her fingers lower between us, tracing the exposed skin at the top of my panties, her mouth pulling back from mine, waiting for approval. I nodded, pulling her lips back to mine as her hand dipped below the fabric. Her fingertips roamed between my thighs, and I pushed against her touch, not able to get enough of her.

I moaned into Cara's mouth as I slid her shirt up her stomach and over her chest, palming her breast as she had done to mine, making her whimper into my mouth. It was the sexiest sound I'd ever heard, and I wanted to make her do it over and over again.

Her hand left my panties just long enough to shove them down my hips, and I slid off her to kick them down my legs as she pulled her tank top over her head and her fingers looped into her own underwear.

"Wait," I put my hand on hers, and she froze. Her face looked panicked, as if I was suddenly deciding I no longer wanted her. That couldn't be further from the truth. Pulling my tank top over my head, her gaze fell to my exposed breasts as my hair cascaded down over my shoulders. I pulled my lip between my teeth and grabbed her underwear, slowly exposing her silky flesh. She let out a heavy sigh as she lifted her feet so I could free them from the fabric. My eyes danced over her beautiful body, and I still couldn't believe that someone as incredible as Cara wanted *me*.

I leaned back over her and pressed my lips to hers as her fingers tangled in my hair, rolling herself on top of me with one of her thighs between mine.

Feeling her bare skin against mine was almost too much to handle. Shivers rocked my body as her hips rolled against mine, her small breasts pressed against my chest.

"Does that feel good?"

"Yes." I moaned, lost in her touch.

Her mouth traveled down, pressing against my neck. I felt her tongue slide over my skin, and my body bucked, craving more. She continued the trail of kisses down my shoulder and across my clavicle as she slid lower.

Pulling my nipple in between her lips, her tongue flicked over its hardened peak. Her fingers slid down between my legs as she pressed against my clit, sending a shockwave of pleasure through me. I turned my head to the side, pressing my cheek against the cool pillow, my eyes falling closed as I enjoyed the moment.

"You're so beautiful," she whispered against my skin, her breath against my stomach causing me to shiver as she climbed between my parted thighs. I glanced down at Cara as her emerald eyes locked onto mine through her thick lashes, her lips pressed to my skin just below my belly button.

My body was on fire as I watched her lips travel over my mound, fluttering kisses and dragging her tongue over me. As her mouth finally made it between my thighs a shiver rocked through my body; goose bumps erupted all over my flesh. I reached down between my legs and ran my fingers through her hair as her tongue ran over where I needed her most.

"Cara," I whimpered as she pushed my legs farther apart.

"I won't hurt you," she assured me as her tongue ran over me again, pressing her finger inside of me. I arched my back, desperate to be as close to her as possible. Her finger moved in and out of my body at a lazy pace as she continued to torment me with her mouth.

"That feels so good." I panted as she slid a second finger inside of me. "I'm going to come." I could feel my cheeks heat. Even with what we were doing, I was embarrassed by my words.

"I want us to come together."

Cara crawled up between my thighs, a seductive smile on her lips before she lowered her body against mine. As soon as our lips touched it was like a fire ignited in my veins. I could taste my excitement on her lips, and I wanted to taste hers as well. I tangled my fingers in her hair, desperate to deepen our kiss. Her right thigh slid over my left, and she rocked against me, causing her damp flesh to slide over mine. I moaned into her mouth as I pressed back against her, and my free hand slipped between us to palm her breast. Pressure began to build deep in my belly. Our panting grew louder as I took my hand from her chest and grabbed her ass, pulling her harder against me.

"Don't stop," I begged, breathless.

She whimpered as both of our bodies began to tremble, and pleasure rolled through us like waves crashing against the shore. She wrapped her arms around me and held me tightly as she struggled to catch her breath, panting in my ear, our bodies slick with sweat.

CHAPTER TWENTY

Cara

I lay awake for hours watching Ellie's chest rise and fall as she slept, my heart crumbling, knowing that this probably didn't mean as much to her as it did to me. Even if it did, fate once again was intervening, and I'd be pulled away from her before we even had a chance to see what it could be.

I let the tears flow, dampening the pillow beneath my cheek. I had to say my good-byes now, because when the time came for me to leave, I wouldn't be able to find the words. I tucked El's hair behind her ear and pressed a kiss to her temple. She stirred and rolled onto her side. Inching closer, I slid my arm around her waist, pulling her back against my chest.

I lay unmoving until the sun poured through the window, and I reluctantly had to let go of her. I dressed quietly and snuck back into my room, staring at the ceiling until I heard David and Dawn moving around the house.

My body was exhausted, but my brain refused to slow down. I hadn't said a civil word to my mother since she kicked me out, and now I had to summon the courage to beg for her forgiveness. The idea made me ill.

A knock at the door caused the panic in my head to silence as Dawn opened it and stuck her head inside. "I made breakfast."

"I'm not hungry." I stared up at the ceiling refusing to look at her. She sighed loudly as she leaned against the doorframe.

"I want you to know that this wasn't my idea."

"It's fine. I'm fine." But it hurt to confirm that she had spoken to David about me leaving.

"David is just worried about his daughter."

A single tear fell down my cheek and disappeared into my hair. "So am I. Her own father barely acknowledges her existence." I looked over at her now. She wasn't angry. She looked like she understood, and it made me feel guilty for making her feel uncomfortable. The idea made me laugh, because I hadn't realized how much Ellie had rubbed off on me. I wished David and Dawn could see that positive effect she'd had on me.

"Come eat."

"I have some things to do this morning…but thanks for the offer."

She smiled sadly, pulling my door closed behind her. I heard her take a few steps down the hall and knock on Ellie's door. They spoke for a moment, but I couldn't make out what they were saying before two sets of footsteps descended the stairs.

When I knew no one else was on the second floor I grabbed my phone and called my mother. The phone rang three times before she answered, sounding annoyed.

"Mom," I said, clearing my throat as a million thoughts flew through my mind. I wanted to tell her she was wrong about me, that I would find love, and I had. I felt it from the moment I first laid eyes on Ellie. "We need to talk."

I made plans to meet my mother later today, and I couldn't stop from pacing my floor, changing my clothes at least ten times to find something overly feminine to help sell the lie that I was no longer the gay child she should be embarrassed about.

As the clock ticked away, the minutes seeming to wear down fast, I hurried downstairs. My body jolted to a stop as I laid eyes on Ellie, her hair wavy and wild. She was wearing the clothes she'd worn last night. She looked like she'd spent all night making love, and I couldn't help the rush of knowing it had been with me.

I wanted to walk across the room and kiss her deeply. Instead, I looked over at David who was eyeing me wearily.

"I'm volunteering today," I lied as I avoided Ellie's narrowed gaze.

"Have fun," Dawn called from the fridge where she was bent over, searching for something on a bottom shelf.

I walked toward the front door as I heard a chair scrape against the hardwood floor, but I refused to look back.

"Wait, you said I could come volunteer with you if I wanted," Ellie called from behind me. I stopped, not turning around.

"I'll have to talk to someone at the hospital first." I pulled open the front door and stepped on the porch. Ellie caught it before it could close.

She stepped out behind me and closed the door so David and Dawn could not hear our conversation. "You said you didn't go to the hospital anymore."

I turned around to face her, torturing myself further. I clenched my fists at my sides, begging my body to stay put and not go to her.

"I just have some things to take care of today." I gave her a small smile.

"Okay," she grinned back as she tucked her hair behind her ear.

I hurried down the steps and down the driveway. I could feel her eyes on me, and I knew when I slid into Tristan's passenger seat that her heart must have been crumbling like mine.

But if I wanted to sell the lie to my mother of how I'd changed, that I was only experimenting when I was younger, I needed Tristan there to prove it and act as a buffer. I knew my mom wouldn't bring up what I had done in front of a stranger. She was far too ashamed of me.

"So where are we going?" Tristan asked as he ran his hand over my bare thigh. I was wearing a pleated white skirt and multitoned purple argyle sweater. I put my hand on his to stop him from moving it farther up my leg.

"We are going to meet my mother." My head jerked slightly as he tapped the brakes, but I kept my eyes ahead.

"Your what? Babe, you told me your mother was dead." I let go of his hand and dug my nails into my palms. I thought of the tangle of lies that would slowly become unraveled if I didn't keep my stories straight.

"I didn't say that *exactly*, you just assumed. You never really asked, actually."

"Are you fucking kidding me right now? I smoked a bowl like twenty minutes ago. I can't go meet your fucking mom you told me was dead."

"My mom abandoned me, okay? I don't like to talk about it. But I want to make things right with her. I have to. So please just come along. I promise it will be quick and painless." I chanced a glance over at him. His jaw was clenched, and I knew he was pissed, but right now I had no other choice. "I'll make it up to you." The idea of what he would expect in return made me sick to my stomach.

I directed Tristan to Corleone's Restaurant just outside of town. As we stood at the hostess's stand, my knees almost gave out when I saw my mother sitting at a table in the far right corner. She looked exactly like I'd remembered her, but tired. Her long chestnut hair was pulled into a neat bun. I knew this time apart must have been hard for her, but I hated myself for feeling sorry for her.

"There she is." I grabbed Tristan's hand and began to pull him toward her table, feeling like I was walking to my own execution. In a way, I was. If all went well, I'd have to say good-bye to who I truly was and live a lie.

"Mom." I nodded, and her eyes went to Tristan, widening almost as if she was a cartoon, and soon they would pop out of her head. "This is my boyfriend, Tristan." I smiled, feeling like a sleaze after the night I'd had with Ellie, but I had to say good-bye to her now. Soon, I'd be saying good-bye to Tristan as well. I'd thought maybe I could stay with him, but after what had happened, I knew it wasn't a good idea. I didn't want to continue things with him now that I knew what my heart truly wanted.

"Pleasure to meet you, Tristan. Please call me Meredith." She smiled as she waved for us to sit down across from her.

I sank down in my chair, tugging on Tristan's hand so he would sit as well.

"This is a pleasant surprise. Cara hadn't told me she was seeing someone."

CHAPTER TWENTY-ONE
Ellie

As the hours slowly crept by, panic settled in my chest, but I knew that breaking up with Tristan would be really hard on Cara. I didn't expect her to be back for a while.

My father was home from work today, and he seemed much more relaxed around me. He even ordered pizza for lunch, and we watched a movie together, but I couldn't pay attention to the story line. My mind kept drifting to Cara. It would be so weird telling my dad that she and I were dating, but he seemed like he would be understanding. I know they didn't get along well, but that would all change once he knew how much I loved her. My heart swelled as I repeated the words in my head. *I am in love with her.*

I still didn't know him very well, but he did take me in, and he took in Cara when she needed a place to stay. My stomach turned when I realized I still didn't know why. She kept so many secrets from everyone, and I hoped that when I told her how I felt she would let down her walls.

"What's wrong?" David's voice interrupted my thoughts.

"Nothing." I focused on the television.

"You were frowning."

I fought against a smile as I remembered Cara telling me I wore my emotions on my face.

"What happened with you and Mom?" I hadn't meant to ask, but I'd just sort of blurted it out. I wanted a chance to be closer to him, and I couldn't do that without knowing why he walked out on us.

He groaned, leaning forward as he rested his elbows on his knees, and his head hung low. "I don't want to talk about your mother."

"Well, I do." I sat forward, and he lifted his head to look at me.

"I have a right to know."

"I know you hate me, Elise."

"I don't hate you, David. I had a wonderful life with Mom. She was all I needed."

He flinched, but he needed to understand that I didn't suffer from him not being there. Yes, it would have been great to have him around, and I was always envious of the other kids at school who had two parents, but I didn't suffer.

"I guess I deserve that." His eyes studied my face. "You look just like her, you know."

"Thanks," I smiled, tucking my hair behind my ear. "I'm not mad, David. I just need to know."

He ran his hand over his jaw as he let out a deep sigh. "I loved your mother. We'd known each other all through college. But things were different back then."

"Different how?" I leaned closer to him as if I'd hear the truth sooner that way.

"We were young and stupid, Ellie."

"Everyone is stupid when they're young."

He laughed, shaking his head as he leaned back against the couch. "It was worse back then. I really don't want to go into details." Clearing his throat, he wrung his hands as he struggled to find the words. "Your mother was dating my best friend."

His revelation knocked the air from my lungs, and I gasped audibly. Was my mother cheating on her boyfriend? That seemed so out of character for her. "You… weren't dating her?"

"No. Not then. Eric was a great guy, and he treated your mother the way she deserved to be treated. Even though I had feelings for her, I never acted on them when they were together."

"So what happened?"

"Senior year, he was driving down from the lake where we usually spent the weekends. He'd been drinking, and when he took a curve too fast, he overcompensated and slid into oncoming traffic."

I placed my hand over my mouth, shocked at what I was hearing, but still uncertain how this had anything to do with me.

"Your mother wasn't in the car, thank God. She had stayed behind to play volleyball on the beach. I was her ride home." He hung his head again, shaking it as the memories of what had transpired began to upset him. "We didn't find out that he'd been in an accident until a few hours later when we made it back to the dorms. He was killed instantly. He didn't suffer."

"Okay," I whispered as I placed my hand on his arm, encouraging him to continue. "Is that when you guys began dating?"

"No. Your mom was heartbroken over Eric. She wouldn't go to class or eat anything. But then, two months later, everything changed."

His eyes met mine as if hoping I'd understand. "What happened?" I was on the edge of the couch cushion now.

"She found out that she was pregnant with Eric's child."

I pulled my hand from his arm as if I'd been shocked. "He was my father?"

David nodded. "I tried to be there for her. I took care of her as if I were her boyfriend and your father. Eventually we did begin to date and planned to marry, but she never got over Eric. She would cry in her sleep. It killed me that she was hurting so badly, but it was also killing me to know that she would never love me as she loved him. I would never have been good enough for her. She had already found her soul mate."

"I can't believe this."

"I never wanted to leave you. Believe me, if I thought there was ever a chance that she and I could make it work, I would have stayed. But I knew I had to move on and find love for myself."

What he said made sense, but it didn't make the truth any easier to swallow. All this time I had thought he left my mom and caused her to struggle, but it was he who had suffered, trying to love someone who could never love him back.

I heard the front door open and close. My heart rate began to pick up, and I felt like every nerve ending in my body was vibrating with anticipation. When Dawn stuck her head around the corner, it felt like I'd been kicked in the gut. The work day was already over, and Cara still wasn't home. She'd been out for hours, and I was embarrassed to admit to myself that I missed her and worried that she was still with Tristan. I needed to tell her what I'd learned about my father, who wasn't really my father at all. As the truth began to settle over me, I realized Cara was all I had. My entire life had been a lie.

Dawn sat down next to my father, and my skin felt like it was crawling as I waited for them to get ready to go see the fireworks downtown for the local Fourth of July celebration. I'd forgotten it was even a holiday with all of my panicking. The movie ended, and we were partway through a cooking show when I finally excused myself so I could go to my room and lose my mind in peace. I paced the floor, chewing my nails, pausing only to look out of my bedroom window whenever a headlight from a car flashed in the distance. I needed Cara so badly right then; I was physically aching with her absence.

I dug through my purse and pulled out my prepaid cell phone. I hardly used it and still had my twenty dollars' worth of minutes on it from when I first moved in with David; he insisted I have one for emergency purposes. The only person I'd call would be Cara, and since we were always together, I never needed it.

I scrolled to her number and began to type out a text message, erasing and retyping it three times before deciding on "Hey. What's up?" I hit send, immediately regretting what I'd typed as I clutched the phone in my palm and began to pace again. After fifteen excruciatingly long minutes, and my father popping his head in to say they were leaving and inviting me to go along with them, I decided to find her for myself. Cara once told me if I wanted something I should take it. I couldn't go another minute without confessing how I felt about her. She was the only person I felt like I truly belonged to.

I hurried around my room, changing my clothes and making myself look presentable in a pale-blue sundress and brown strappy sandals. My cheeks hurt from smiling so much. I knew Cara was probably upset over having to end things with Tristan, but once I was able to hold her in my arms, I knew I could take all of that pain away.

I scrolled down through the numbers on my phone and sent a quick text to Brody asking where he was. He responded a minute later, telling me he was hanging out with his brother Luke. I asked if there was any way for him to come get me as I slipped out of the front door into the warm night air. As soon as I was halfway down the driveway, I hit the call button so I could talk to Brody without trying to text and walk.

"Hey, El. Where's your sidekick?" he asked as the stones made a crunching noise below my feet.

"She's with Tristan. I figured you'd be with them," I replied casually.

"Nah. He called earlier. They went out to dinner or some shit with her mom and then hit a party at the swimming hole for the Fourth of July. Tris has been kind of a dick lately, and I didn't feel like putting up with his shit."

My heart sank. She took Tristan to meet her mother? Why? Did he know why she was living with David, but I didn't? Of course he did. He was her boyfriend.

"You there?" Brody asked in my ear as I wrapped my free arm around my waist. Tristan must have been lying. Cara and I had something together, and he was probably too ashamed to tell Brody that he'd been dumped. I began to worry that maybe he'd lost his growing temper with Cara. He'd been acting increasingly cruel toward her, even if she denied it.

"Yeah. Yeah. Sorry. I was just trying to figure out which way to walk," I lied as I turned left out of the driveway.

"You want me to come get you? We can hang out and watch the fireworks."

"Um…actually, do you think you could take me to the swimming hole?"

"Sure. Yeah. I guess we could check it out for a little while. You can see the fireworks from there."

I smiled, loving that Brody was such a good friend. I knew he had a crush on me, and had I not been so into Cara, I wouldn't have minded dating him. Under his party persona he was a really kind and funny guy, nothing like Tristan claimed.

"I'll be walking down Main Street," I told him before we said our good-byes.

As soon as we hung up, I checked my messages again. If Cara was swimming, she probably had no idea I'd even sent her a message in the first place. My heart rate finally began to slow as I paced down the crowded sidewalk. All of the stores were long closed for the festivities, except for Chewy's Bar. A few drunks spilled into the street, smoking outside because it was illegal to do so in the business. I ignored the catcalls of a few guys and crossed the street, thankful when a blue Civic slowed to a stop beside me. I saw Brody's crooked smile.

I pulled open the passenger door and slid in, and then we took off down the road.

"I was surprised you called me," he confessed, glancing over at me. His gaze dropped to my bare legs before looking back at my face.

"Well, we're usually all together," I reminded him as I looked out of the front window.

"Yeah. Tristan has been kind of shitty lately. You avoiding him, too?"

"I think everyone is at this point." I ran my fingers through my hair.

"Everyone except Cara."

"I think she's tired of him, too," I confessed, immediately regretting what I'd said.

"Oh, really?" His smirk grew as he waited for me to elaborate with some juicy gossip.

"I mean, she has to be, right?" I turned the volume knob on the radio. "Oh, I love this song," I lied.

We pulled into the dirt road that led to the swimming hole. There were four cars parked just outside of the tree line. My heart began to race again as I unbuckled my seat belt and opened my door. Brody jogged around to my side and draped his arm over my shoulders as he guided me through the darkened path toward the clearing beside the water. There was a small bonfire, and as I stared through the flames, I saw Cara, who was sitting on Tristan's lap. She was turned sideways, her lips on his as they kissed passionately, not caring who was around to see. As her mouth, which had explored my body only the night before, left his, her eyes locked onto mine. I could see them widen a bit before she smiled, pretending to laugh at a joke Cameron was telling.

I'd rather have been stabbed in the back a thousand times than to have to look Cara in the eye when she broke my heart. The pain was crippling, and I let a tear roll down my cheek, unable to take my eyes off her. *Don't you know how much you mean to me? Can't you feel how much I love you?*

Brody pulled me down beside him on an old log, his arm loosely around my waist as his fingers tapped an unknown beat on my hip.

He began speaking to the others, but all I could hear was the blood whooshing through my ears as I tried not to pass out from the ache in my chest. But then Cara spoke, and my head snapped up to see her looking directly at me, while she was responding to Brody.

"It wasn't like that, Bro. We just had dinner with my mom. It'd been a long time since I'd seen her, and I didn't want to go alone."

I wanted to scream that I would have gone with her. I would have been there for her. Maybe she was worried her mom would be able to tell something was going on between us, and she wasn't ready to tell her that yet, with their strained relationship. I did show my emotions on my face, as Cara had told me when I'd first met her. I'm sure her mother would have noticed how in love with her daughter I was as soon as she saw me. *But if I really did do that, couldn't Cara see how much I was hurting now? Does what others think mean more than me?*

She smiled sadly at me, and I knew she was trying to put my mind at ease, but she was still on Tristan's lap, and she had been kissing him.

"You want a beer?" Brody asked.

"Yes, please."

He smirked before grabbing us each a beer from the cooler. Cameron held out a bottle of clear liquor, and I took it without even bothering to read the label to see what it was. I poured the liquid fire down my throat, struggling not to cough as it ran down my chin, disappearing into the fabric of my dress.

Brody took the bottle as I pulled it from my lips and quickly replaced it with a can of beer. I greedily drank it down, trying to wash away the flavor of the cheap vodka.

"Whoa, easy." He pulled the bottle from my mouth and wiped my chin with the pad of his thumb before sticking it in his mouth. Tipping the vodka to his lips, he drank a swig, his eyes never leaving mine.

My head grew foggy as I took another drink of my beer and tried to focus on Cameron's story and not on

Cara. But it was impossible not to let my gaze drift to her, and my heart broke all over again each time I did. I struggled internally for the next hour. I wanted to yell at her and pull her away from him. At the same time, I wanted to walk away and never look back.

Maybe she was waiting for school to start for him to end things with her. That was only a few weeks away, but it felt like a lifetime. Maybe she wanted me to make the first move. I hadn't exactly confessed my love for her last night, although I'm sure she knew how important what we'd done together was for me.

But my self-doubt struggled to fight through the fog of alcohol and convince me that it was because last night meant nothing to Cara.

There was only one way to find out, and as Brody held out the bottle of vodka to me, the flames made his eyes sparkle. I wrapped my fingers around the neck of the bottle, over his, and I leaned into him. His lips found mine, and he didn't hesitate to slide his tongue over them. I let my mouth fall open, granting him access. He was gentler than Tristan, but confident. When he pulled back, his eyes searching mine, I smiled shyly, not believing I'd allowed myself to do that. But love makes you do crazy things, and a broken heart makes you not care about the consequences. I glanced up through the flames to see Cara's face now reflecting the sadness I felt deep in my chest. I hated myself for hurting her, even if she'd done the same to me.

I couldn't look at her again as the night wore on, and the flames began to die down in the fire and in my heart.

I had no choice but to sit there and pretend to be happy, as if my entire world wasn't crumbling around me. I had no one.

Even worse, I'd have to sleep one thin wall away from her, in the very bed we'd made love in.

"You want to get out of here?" Brody whispered in my ear, his vodka breath fanning over my cheek and making my stomach turn. The flames blurred now, and I could see two of Cara retreating into the woods with two Tristans. I blinked, rubbing my hands over my eyes as I tried to make the world come into focus again.

"Stay," I mumbled. "I want you to stay."

Brody chuckled as he placed his fingers under my chin and turned me to face him. "I wasn't going to go anywhere without you." It took me a moment to realize he'd thought I was speaking to him.

"Where are they going?" I asked as I looked back at the trees that Tristan and Cara had disappeared through.

"They went to spend some time alone together."

"To talk?"

He laughed as he looked to my lips. "I doubt they will be doing much talking."

My stomach rolled as my world began to spin. "Take me home with you."

The last thing I remembered was telling Brody to take me home. As I opened my eyes and pried his heavy arm off my body, tears sprang to my eyes. I slid out from under him, my hand covering my mouth as I shook my head, begging the tears not to fall. Brody's eyes cracked open, and he rolled to his back, stretching his arms over his head.

"It's like six in the morning, El. Come back to bed."

"Oh my God. I have to get home before my dad… David gets up. He's going to kill me."

"All right. I'm up. Fuck," he mumbled as he rubbed the palm of his hand against his eye.

As he stood my eyes scanned his nearly naked body. He was wearing a pair of black boxer briefs and the intricate tribal tattoo that ran down his muscular arm.

"I don't remember anything," I squealed as he turned around to face me. His brow furrowed before he seemed to understand what I was thinking. He grabbed his jeans and stepped into them.

"Jesus Christ, El. I like you, but I'm not a fucking rapist." He waved his hand toward me, and I looked down, sighing when I realized I was fully clothed. Pulling a T-shirt over his head, he rolled his neck, releasing some of the tension in his muscles.

"I'm sorry," I rubbed my hand over my forehead, my head was pounding with each beat of my panicked heart. "I didn't mean to accuse you of anything."

He shook his head, dismissing my apology. "It's fine. You woke up in a strange bed after drinking too much. I'd be worried if you didn't care how you'd gotten here."

"You're a good guy, Bro."

"I know. It's one of my many flaws," he said with a smile as he grabbed his keys and wallet from the nightstand beside his bed before stepping into his sneakers.

I followed him out of the house and to his car just as the sun was beginning to rise and the air was already warm.

My father and Dawn had off today because everyone in town was out celebrating Independence Day. I was praying that meant they'd be sleeping in, and I'd be able to slip into my room unnoticed.

We rode in silence for a few minutes as I watched the clouds turn pink and purple.

"So, how much of last night *do* you remember?" he asked, and I looked down at my hands as I wrung them.

"I remember that I'll never drink vodka again," I joked, and he laughed as he turned down another street. "And I remember kissing you." I glanced over at him as he looked at me, smiling.

"I was hoping you wouldn't forget that."

There was so much I wished I had forgotten.

"Thanks for hanging out with me and letting me stay over."

"Anytime." His smile widened, and I couldn't help but giggle. "Of course you can stay over whenever you want, but that's not what I meant." He cleared his throat and looked away as if he was embarrassed. He wasn't anything like the womanizing jerk Tristan had always painted him to be. Fuck Tristan.

I reached over and wrapped my fingers around his hand that rested on his thigh, giving it a small squeeze. "Thank you."

He looked down at our hands before weaving his fingers in mine. It was comforting, but I couldn't help but feel like I was cheating on Cara somehow. Blurred visions of her retreating into the woods with Tristan assaulted my memory, and I had to squeeze my eyes closed to try to force them from my memory. I pulled my hand free from Brody's and ran my fingers roughly through my hair.

"What's wrong?"

I shook my head before slowly opening my eyes. "Brody, I did something…I don't even know how to say it." I laughed nervously as I looked out the passenger window. I couldn't look at his face as I confessed what I'd done. My eyes welled up with tears as I thought of everything Cara and I had done together.

"You can talk to me, El. What happened?"

I turned to see the concern on his face as he pulled the car off to the side of the road and put it in park so he could give me his undivided attention.

"I…ugh…I lied to you about something."

I wrung my hands as I lost all of my courage. I couldn't look into his caramel eyes and tell him I'd kissed him because I was upset over Cara. I couldn't tell anyone our secret when I didn't know where we stood anymore. So I confessed a smaller lie.

"I'm not starting college this year. I'm going to be a senior. I won't be eighteen for a while." I braced for him to scream and tell me I was a jerk.

He blew out a deep breath and shook his head, running his hand over the back of his head. "That's…that's kind of crazy, El. We've had you to all of these parties. We drank with you. I mean. I kissed you. Fuck. I kissed you and had you sleep in my bed." His voice was calm, and he seemed to be racking his brain to see which of our transgressions was worse. I was a horrible person.

"I'm so sorry, Bro." I pulled on the door handle and it popped open.

"Wait. Where are you going? We're still a half mile from your place."

"I figured you'd want me to go."

"Why? I mean, it sucks you lied. I really wish I had known your age before I..." he shook his head and laughed. "Just close the door."

I pulled the door closed as he put the car in drive and continued down the road.

"Do you hate me?"

"No. I don't hate you, El. I very strongly...*don't* hate you."

I giggled, shaking my head as he pulled up to the end of my driveway. "I very much don't hate you either. Thanks for the ride."

I smiled over at him one last time before getting out and wandering down the driveway. I was in no hurry to get inside and find out if I would be grounded for the rest of my life.

I slipped in the front door with my sandals in my hands and tiptoed across the living room and up the stairs. I sighed with relief as I snuck into my room and closed the door behind me. When I turned around, I yelped as I saw Cara sitting on the foot of my bed.

"What are you doing in here?" I dropped my shoes on the floor beside me, afraid to step closer to her.

"Making sure you made it home safely, but I see Brody took good care of you." She stood as she walked toward me, shaking her head with a look of disappointment on her face. I held my breath as she reached me, but she only stepped around me and went out of the door, closing it quietly behind her.

My heart crumbled all over again as I fell back against my door. How had I suddenly become the bad guy? My sadness quickly turned to anger, and I left my room, yanking open her door as she turned to look at me, shocked.

"What are you doing?" she asked angrily.

"Fuck you, Cara."

"We did that already, El." She placed her hands on her hips as her eyes narrowed.

"Add it to my long list of regrets."

"Is Brody on that list now, too?"

"You have no right to say *anything* about Brody. After you slept with me, you took Tris to meet your fucking mom, who I still know nothing about, then you drug him off to fuck him in the woods."

Cara stepped toward me, her voice low. "I took Tristan to meet my mom because he's my boyfriend. That's what girlfriends and boyfriends do. And you have no idea what happened in those woods."

"That's what they do, huh? So Tristan introduced you to his mom now, too, or is he still too ashamed of you?"

Cara stuck her finger in my face, and I could see she was struggling to keep herself quiet enough not to wake David. "You have no right to judge me."

"You're right. To judge you, I'd have to actually know you, and no one knows who the real Cara is, do they? You're a real good fucking liar." I turned away from her and gripped the doorknob before looking over my shoulder at her one last time. "For the record, I don't regret *anything* with Brody. I only regret loving *you*." With that, I left her, never looking back as tears ran down my cheeks.

CHAPTER TWENTY-TWO

Cara

My heart broke on a Tuesday. She loved me. She loved *me*, and it killed me inside. I picked up my phone as I sank down on the edge of my bed, and called the one person I knew could make all of this go away.

"Mom, I'm ready to come home. I don't need time to pack."

"I thought you wanted to stay at David's for your birthday."

"No. I want to spend it with you and Dad."

I could hear her exhale into the receiver. "I'm sure your father would like that, Cara. We've been praying that you'd come to your senses. This has been so hard for us. We're both so proud of you. Your boyfriend is a good Christian man."

"Thanks, Mom." Bile rose in my throat. She would never see Tristan again.

"I can come by and get you after my nail appointment at lunch."

"That's…perfect."

Tears rolled down my face, and I didn't bother to wipe them away. I told my mother I loved her and began to pack a few of my belongings into an old duffel bag. There wasn't much that I wanted to take with me. I wanted to forget these last few months and move on with my newest lie, pretending I didn't care.

Ellie might hate me now, but she'd thank me one day. She wouldn't be turned away by her family and forced to start again. Brody would be good to her. Taking Tristan into the woods to confess to him that I wasn't going to be starting college was hard, but when we returned and watched Ellie and Brody leave together, I knew she would be okay without me.

I just wasn't prepared for how much it would hurt. Losing Tatum was nothing compared to the pain of losing Ellie. I'd hoped I'd be long gone before she moved on and I wouldn't have to witness it. At least now I knew I was doing the right thing. David wanted me gone, and I couldn't have him disown his own daughter after she'd lost her mother so recently. She needed this second chance with him.

I smiled as I thought of her still having my e-reader. She would have hundreds of books to get lost in, and I could see what she was reading online anytime I wanted, and even add to the collection. It was small, but being able to have that one connection with her felt like it would help.

I took my bag and glanced around my room one last time before I snuck downstairs and slipped out of the front door before anyone knew I was gone.

I carried my small sack of belongings down the long driveway, feeling like I was leaving a piece of myself behind. But life is nothing more than a series of compromises and picking up the pieces after your world comes crashing down around you. I was good at adapting. I would make this work until I was able to earn enough money to move out on my own.

I didn't exactly make the best choices when I was forced to move in with Dawn and David. I was hurt, and my heart was broken. Because of those poor choices, I was leaving their house feeling the same way, but the only person I could blame was myself.

I walked to the library and grabbed a paperback copy of *The Good Girls*, getting lost in the pages, as I waited for my mother to take me away to my new life. But I couldn't get through a chapter without my tears falling onto the page.

I never expected Ellie to forgive me for leaving this way, but telling her that her father was forcing us apart seemed like it would be too much for her to handle.

Tristan had texted me four times since I stepped foot in the library. He called me everything from Lolita to a frigid bitch for not fucking him one last time in the woods.

"Oh, *Lolita*. I'll have to check that book out before I leave," I mumbled to myself as I heard a quiet chuckle behind me. I spun around to see a girl about my age with short blond hair and legs that went on for miles.

"*The Good Girls*," she said as she nodded in approval. "Do you always talk to your books about what other books you want to read? Aren't you worried they'll get jealous?"

"You're a smartass," I quipped as I noticed her eyes looking over my body as if she was imagining covering my flesh with her tongue. "Actually, I was just reading a text from my boyfriend," I held up my phone to show her.

"Oh. Well, I'll let you get back to it." With a small wave of her finger, she disappeared through the shelves, and I returned to my book, hoping that time would move more quickly.

CHAPTER TWENTY-THREE

Ellie

When Cara disappeared, she took a piece of me with her, the piece that held my will to live. I barely ate and refused to get out of bed. I'd never felt so alone in my life. I ignored all calls and messages until one day, there was a knock at my bedroom door. When I didn't respond, it cracked open.

"How long are you going to avoid everyone?"

I rolled over, shocked to hear Brody's voice in my house.

"How did you get in here?"

"Your dad let me in." He smiled as he took a few steps closer to my bed, his eyes dancing around the room. I wanted to correct him and tell him that David was not my father, but it didn't really matter.

"Really?"

"Why wouldn't he?" He put his hand on his chest and pretended he was offended. "I'm a good guy."

"You are," I sighed and curled into a ball on my side.

"You want to get out of here and maybe get some lunch?"

"Not today," I tried to give him a small smile, but my lip quivered as thoughts of *her* came flashing back.

"You must really miss Cara." He wasn't asking, simply observing. I nodded my head as he walked over to the edge of my bed and sank down on his haunches so he was eye level. "You can't keep yourself locked away like this, El. It's not good for you, and it won't get better if you don't try."

"I don't want to try."

"Well, you don't have a choice. I miss you."

"You're not missing out on much."

"You know, that first night at the party when I saw you kiss Cara, I thought to myself, I wish that girl would look at me the way she's looking at her. Silly, right?"

"That is silly. It was just a stupid kiss."

His eyes narrowed as he brushed my hair from my forehead. "Because I knew right then that you'd never look at anyone else the way you looked at her. I saw it from day one. And I saw what it did to you on the Fourth of July."

"I don't know what you're talking about."

"Yes you do. And it must be really hard not being able to talk to anyone about it. I don't think Cara had anyone to talk to either."

"I don't think Cara gave a shit about anyone but herself."

He laughed sadly and held out his hand to me. Reluctantly I placed my palm in his and let him pull me to my feet.

"I don't think that's true."

I looked to the ground between us as I felt the tears began to fill my eyes. "Where do you want to go?" I asked as I tugged at my T-shirt.

"Dawn said she has been trying to get you to go school shopping. Maybe I could take you. I'm not good with girl clothing, but I'll tell you your ass looks great in whatever you try on."

I smiled for the first time in weeks. I hadn't given school a second thought. I haven't given anything a second thought after Cara disappeared.

I ran my fingers through my lilac-scented hair and pulled it up into a messy ponytail before slipping my hand back in his and letting him guide me down the stairs. Dawn and David were in the kitchen talking, and both of their voices cut off as they looked to us.

I tried to pull my hand free from Brody's, but he held it tight in his as we walked toward them. My heart felt like it was going to explode, but Brody wasn't afraid at all.

David reached in his back pocket and pulled out some cash, handing it over to Brody. "Make sure she comes back with everything she needs," he said with a smile, and I couldn't help but grin back at him.

"Thanks, David."

"Don't bring her back too late," he warned Brody, who assured them both he would take good care of me.

We shopped for hours, and I had nearly everything I needed, thanks to Brody keeping a list of the essentials such as packs of gum and rubber bands to shoot at people.

We ended up in the food court of the mall with bags piled around us. For the first time in weeks, I felt like I was starving, and my cheeks actually hurt from smiling, but I still felt empty inside. I knew it would take time to fill that void, but I was thankful Brody was willing to help me along that journey.

Halfway through my second slice of pizza, I nearly choked on a pepperoni when I noticed Tristan. He looked at me quizzically for a moment before he sauntered over to our table, a blonde tucked under his arm.

"Long time, no see, El." He nodded his chin toward me, and I struggled to swallow against the lump in my throat. The last thing I wanted to do was talk to Cara's ex-boyfriend. But when my eyes flicked to the girl under his arm, I felt the insane need to defend her that was now more prevalent than my jealousy toward him.

"Not that long. What's it been? Three weeks, maybe, since Cara left?"

He shrugged, shifting his stance like I'd made him uncomfortable. Good. "She shouldn't have lied about her age."

The girl cocked an eyebrow, and I struggled not to leap over the table and wipe the painted-on arch off her face.

"You're right about that. She lied about a lot of things."

"Like what?" He was suddenly very open to listening, and I laughed, shaking my head. It was a little late for him to give a shit about who Cara really was.

"Does it matter anymore? You've moved on."

"Just curious."

I struggled not to mention the countless bruises she claimed she'd gotten from running into things or falling, but I didn't have any proof.

"Just leave her alone, Tris." Brody's body tensed beside me, clearly over Tristan's ignorant attitude. I can only imagine how much worse he'd gotten after Cara left him as she did.

"Uh-oh, babe. We've upset the kiddie table. We might get a time-out," Tristan joked to the girl, who laughed at his lame attempt at a joke.

"I wasn't the one screwing a minor." As soon as Brody spoke, both of them shut up, their laughter dying at the awkwardness of his comment, which made me begin to giggle uncontrollably. "What's that old saying? Seventeen will get you twenty?"

"Fuck you, Bro. The only reason you weren't fucking Ellie was because she was too uptight."

"Or she was busy stealing your girlfriend from *you*," Brody shot back and even I couldn't laugh as the tension grew thick between us.

"Okay, Brody. I think it's time for us to go."

"No," Tristan held out his hand for me to wait as I stood. "What the fuck does that mean, Bro?"

Brody sighed as he looked to me. I just shook my head and relaxed back in my seat, preparing for the worst.

"It means, the first night we even took El to a party, your girl shoved her tongue down El's throat."

"Bullshit," Tristan snapped as the girl under his arm took a step away from him, trying to distance herself from the escalating tempers.

"Is it?" Brody cocked his eyebrow as he shoved a french fry in his mouth.

CHAPTER TWENTY-FOUR

Cara

I fell back into my old routine at my mom's house. Even though she had divorced my father a few years ago, he came by nearly every day to help her around the house and spend time with me.

At first it was hard to see Tatum's house without my stomach sinking, but I'd never gotten a glimpse of her. Rumor had it her parents now homeschooled her, and she was spending her summer at church camp.

I begged my mother to let me get my GED so I could begin working and taking college courses online. She hated the thought of me not getting my high school diploma, and I knew I would regret it if I didn't.

I'd thrown myself into working, desperate to begin saving money so I could get out on my own. Waitressing was a hard job, and having to rely on tips made me learn to stifle my sarcastic attitude.

When I wasn't working I would spend every waking moment reading. I didn't want to suffer through a moment of reality, even though I stared at my cell phone constantly. For the first few days after I left, El texted and called me at all hours until I was forced to send David an e-mail, asking him to let her know I'd gone to live with my mother and I was fine. The sooner she moved on and forgot about me the better.

But forgetting about Ellie was impossible. I struggled to smile every day so my mother wouldn't think something was wrong. At church I prayed that Ellie would forgive me, and at night I fantasized about what it would be like to see her again. My mind was in constant turmoil, and my heart was broken without her. What I had for her was just a crush. I knew that now, because losing her absolutely crushed me. I'd died inside when I walked away from her.

I'd come back here because I'd had no other option. I refused to let Ellie stand up for me and alienate herself. I needed to make the best of this opportunity to try to build a future that one day I'd be proud to share with someone else.

I wrote a letter in my journal every day to Ellie, even though I knew she would never get to read them. It made me feel like I still had a connection to her, an invisible thread that tugged on my heart whenever I thought of her beautiful face.

When I first met her I wanted help her come out of her shell and learn to live, but I'd learned so much more from her. I felt loved for the first time—truly loved.

I began to log my every thought, plans for the future, and regrets of the past. If Ellie could see me now, she would laugh at me for becoming so much like she had been when we first met.

CHAPTER TWENTY-FIVE
Ellie

Word spreads quickly in a small town, and I started my senior year with a reputation that preceded me.

It began with a look that lingered a few seconds too long before the whispers began. At first I was certain it was all in my head, but it didn't take long for someone to speak up and let me know that I was going to hell.

By the time I walked into the cafeteria for lunch, I wanted to run out of the school and never look back. Immediately after buying my food, I dumped the tray in the trash and hurried to the bathroom so I could type out a text to Brody.

He reassured me that things would get better over time, and he was right. Every day that he didn't have a class he would drive me to school, kissing me in full view of my classmates before sending me on my way.

The rumors didn't stop, but it did quiet them, and I was able to focus on my schoolwork. Having someone in my corner who wasn't oblivious to who I was made me feel safe for the first time in a long time.

Brody became my protector and my best friend. David was surprisingly lenient when it came to me spending time with him, and I think he was just happy I was no longer lying in bed all day depressed. He didn't have any idea about the rumors at school but after a few weeks, I no longer ate lunch alone. After a few months I had made friends that I hung out with on occasion outside of school because they enjoyed college frat parties. By the end of the school year, I could talk about Cara without crying because I was smiling at Brody. Unfortunately, my grades and attendance suffered because of it.

Brody and I remained just friends, but after my eighteenth birthday, the line began to blur from time to time. I'd never imagined getting over my first love would take so much time. I'd seen my classmates switch partners more often than they'd switch classes and it didn't seem to faze them at all. Maybe they were better at hiding their true feelings, as Cara had been.

One thing I learned over time is that I didn't care what they thought of me. I embraced the rumors and became the wild child they all thought I was. I became Cara McCarthy, and I never felt more alone.

CHAPTER TWENTY-SIX
Cara

As hard as I'd tried to avoid having to face the world again, I was actually excited for my first day of high school.

The thought of Ellie, studying and working hard, made me strive to be a better person. One day I hoped to be able to show her what I'd accomplished and that it was all because of her.

Going from being popular to being avoided and talked about was excruciating. In my past I would have started a fight or gone out to get high with the guys, but I didn't have the guys anymore. I didn't have any more chances. Instead, I dove into my work and studied harder than I had ever studied in my life.

When I wasn't focused on school, I plotted out what my next accomplishment would be. I could finally envision a future, and I wanted one that didn't require me to work endless hours and barely able to scrape by. Over time, I realized I wanted to keep my parents in my life. I didn't agree with their views, but I knew their tough-love tactics were because they were afraid of sending me out into the world where everyone would judge me for who I loved.

I kept to myself and finished out my senior year with the best grades I'd ever had. I worked hard, saving money to buy my own car. It barely ran, but with a little work it was reliable enough to take me to and from work and would be perfect for when I left for college.

CHAPTER TWENTY-SEVEN
Ellie

I grabbed the last of my boxes from the closet, looking around my room one last time. I'd changed so much in the little time that I'd lived here. I walked in with a broken heart and no idea of who I really was. Today I'd leave the same way but for a very different reason. I'd lost myself somewhere along the way here, but because of Brody, I was able to struggle through it all and come out the other side relatively unscathed. When I wanted to get lost in the bottom of a bottle of tequila, he forced me to finish my homework. I would never be able to thank him enough for all he'd done for me.

I carried my last two boxes down the stairs and out to the trunk of my red Sundance that I'd gotten for my birthday. David had stayed by my side; even when I struggled to push him from my life, he refused to walk away. I knew he regretted leaving my mother all of those years ago, but I didn't blame him. Loving someone who doesn't love you back is excruciating. He deserved to have his feelings reciprocated. I stopped when I saw him standing by the driver-side door. I knew he had to work today, and I had said my good-byes to him last night, so I was caught off-guard.

"What are you doing home?" I walked to the back of the car, to my open trunk, and frowned. All of my boxes I'd placed in there were now gone. I glanced up at David, who was smiling and holding up a set of keys. I dropped the boxes I held on the ground.

"I don't want you going off with an unreliable vehicle. Leaving us for college is bad enough without having to wonder if you're broken down on the side of the highway."

I smiled as happy tears pricked my eyes. "Thanks, Dad." I walked over to him and wrapped my arms around his waist. We'd come a long way from the strangers we were just a few months ago.

With all of my self-discovery, I'd learned that we all have many sides to us. David wasn't just one thing that he'd done, and he didn't have to be a biological relative to be my dad. He held me tightly against him before pulling back and holding the keys between us.

"The Prius will save you a lot of money on gas."

I grabbed the keys as I looked to his shiny black car. "You love that car."

He smiled as he kicked at the dirt on the driveway. "I love you more. Besides, Dawn and I need something roomier."

"But now it's just the two of you." I narrowed my eyes. He smiled as he waited for what he was saying to click. "You're going to have a baby?" I squealed, hugging him again as we both laughed.

"I wasn't sure how'd you react to that."

"I'm really happy for you both." He released me, clearing his throat, and I knew this good-bye was hard for him. We'd just gotten to be in each other's lives again.

"I'll be home to visit whenever I get the chance. I promise."

He nodded and took a step back from me. I grabbed my final boxes and carried them toward my new car. I shoved the boxes in the back and turned back to look at my father one last time.

"I love you, Dad."

"Love you too, Ellie." He waved, and I slipped into the driver's seat. With a deep breath, I pulled out and headed off to start a new chapter in my life.

It took me two hours to unpack most of my boxes. I'd finally found a place for most of my things and was down to only one last box that was still packed from when I left my mom's. I sat down on my bed and pulled off the packing tape. When I looked inside I gasped, my hand covering my mouth as I let out a sigh.

I could feel warm tears slide down my cheeks as I reached inside the box and pulled out small paper cranes, in various sizes, covered in writing. The box was full of them, and I realized that the writing was my own. These were the scraps of paper from my future plans notebook, which I'd destroyed the first night I'd moved in with my father.

I pulled them out one by one and sat them on my bed. When I'd reached the bottom of the box there was a note.

El,

Someone I love once told me that there is a Japanese legend that says if you make a thousand origami cranes that you will be granted one wish. All I've ever wished for was for someone to love me for who I really am, and I was lucky enough to have you see something in me that was worth your heart.

These cranes are the first step in my very long journey to redemption.

I'm wishing that you will find the kind of love that isn't afraid—the fearless love that you gave me when I didn't deserve it.

Love Always,
Cara

For the first time in weeks, I cried as I thought of Cara, but I wasn't sad. It broke my heart when she left, and I wasn't sure I'd ever understand why she did, but it gave me closure to know that she was trying to change herself.

There was a knock at the door, and I pulled it open to find a girl with short red hair, her nose peppered with freckles.

"Hi. I think I'm your new roommate." Her smile beamed as I stepped to the side and let her enter, followed by an older man who I assumed was her father.

She sat down her bags and turned back to me. "I'm Julie," she held out her hand, and I slid mine into hers.

"I'm Ellie. It's nice to meet you."

Her father was beaming, but his eyes were filled with tears. I knew he was struggling to walk away from his daughter.

"I can help you bring up your boxes if you need an extra hand," I offered, but Julie waved her hand.

"My dad has the rest of my stuff."

As soon as she spoke, another man stepped through the door and set down a stack of boxes. "What did you pack in there, Jules?" he asked with a chuckle as he slipped his arm around the other man.

"I had to bring all of my heels so you don't stretch them out while I'm gone," she joked.

"Ellie," she said as if she suddenly realized I was still in the room. "These are my dads, John and Chris." She pointed to each of them, and I took turns shaking their hands.

"Take care of our girl, Ellie. She's a good girl," Chris said in a mock stern voice, and Julie rolled her eyes and sighed dramatically. I suppressed a giggle, as his words reminded me of my favorite book.

"I'll keep her out of trouble," I promised as I drug my fingers over my chest in a cross motion.

John made a face like he knew I was trouble. Then he shook his head and laughed. "You girls have fun. Just keep each other safe."

I watched as Julie hugged both of her fathers before they left in tears.

"Sorry about that. They are a little overly emotional," she frowned as she pulled open her first box and began to unpack. She glanced over at my bed before looking at me.

"So what was your wish?" she asked as her eyes landed on my paper cranes.

CHAPTER TWENTY-EIGHT

Cara

I sat down on my single-size bed, and I thought of Ellie doing the same at whatever college she ended up at. Knowing we were both adults now and free to do what we wanted tempted me to go to her, but I also knew that she needed a fresh start. I'd put her through hell, and I wasn't naïve. I knew she wasn't going to welcome me with open arms.

My roommate was lying on her stomach, writing in her notebook, wearing only a T-shirt and panties. She rarely spoke, but when she did it was usually to try to diagnose me with some incurable disease she'd found on the Internet. For fun, I started feeding her fake symptoms, but she soon caught on to what I was doing.

I was finally getting the hang of college. I'd done enough partying in high school that it no longer interested me. I studied and worked, with little time for a social life. When I wasn't busy with any of those things, I wrote. At first I kept a journal to help me through losing Ellie, but it took on a life of its own.

Ellie and I had morphed into new characters on the pages, and I finished my first novel a few weeks ago. One day I hoped El would read it so she knew what I had been going through when I'd met her.

I owed her an explanation. I owed her so much more than that. If it weren't for her love, I wouldn't be where I was today. I wasn't ashamed as I was before. I know knew I was worth loving and didn't deserve to be abused.

I struggled every day to save money and get good enough grades to get scholarships. My guidance counselor, Ms. Grable, worked tirelessly to help me become independent so I'd no longer have to hide who I was. She also had my English teacher, Mr. Clark, edit my book, and with their support, I self-published.

It felt freeing to send my story out into the world, in hopes that my words might help someone else who is struggling with who they are. If my suffering could save one person, make them not give up hope, it was all worth it.

CHAPTER TWENTY-NINE
Ellie

It had been six weeks since I'd discovered my box of wishing cranes. I was finally beginning to get into my routine of classes and living on my own, but as I rounded every corner, I searched the crowd for Cara's face. Part of me felt relieved that she was still thinking of me, and part of me hated her for giving me hope and then breaking my heart all over again.

She'd made no effort to contact me again.

It was coming up on the weekend, and I'd promised my father I'd come home for Dawn's birthday. The idea of running into Cara had my nerves shot, but I knew the chances of seeing her were slim.

At least I was able to avoid the inevitable by going to a college four hours away. Once again I was starting over and struggling to discover who I was and wanted to be. Thanks to Julie, that journey had been much easier than I'd expected.

"You ready to meet my dad?" I asked as she pulled on her gray hoodie.

"You did put up with my dads last weekend. I guess it's my turn."

I looked over my room one last time before lacing my fingers in Julie's and pulling her through the door.

The trip was tiring, but I loved having Julie to talk to and distract me from everything I'd left behind.

After Dawn's birthday party, I was exhausted. I spent the next two hours with Julie, cleaning up the mess and washing the dishes. I refused to let the little mama-to-be lift a finger. By the time the house was sparkling, I'd almost burned enough energy to sleep. But as Julie slipped into the bathroom to brush her teeth my eyes fell on Cara's bedroom door.

I stepped inside her deserted room. Her possessions were gone but the furniture remained. I closed the door behind me and sank down on the edge of her bed. I didn't know if my imagination was playing tricks on me, but I swore I could still faintly smell lilacs. I closed my eyes, inhaling the fragrance that haunted my dreams.

I slid off my shoes and curled up on my side, my hand sliding under the pillow and hitting something hard. I pushed myself up and pulled out Cara's e-reader, which she'd left when she moved out. I couldn't keep it, so I put it in her room for her in case she ever returned. I walked over to the dresser and pulled open the top drawer to retrieve the charger cord. I plugged it in, and after a few seconds it powered on. My chest seized as my eyes danced over a new book with a paper crane on the cover called *On a Tuesday*. I clicked the cover, and my eyes blurred when I read the dedication.

For Elise—

Never pretend to be someone you aren't. You are perfect just the way you are.

I held the e-reader to my lips and let another piece of my fractured heart begin to mend.

There was a knock at the door, and I jumped as it slowly opened. Julie looked at me and at the device in my hand.

"What's wrong?" She closed the door, and I suddenly felt like I was suffocating in the small space. I set the e-reader on the dresser before turning to her.

"Can we go for a walk?"

She held out her hand for me, and I let her pull me to my feet. We headed downstairs.

I let Dawn know I would be back before it got too late and gave her a kiss on the cheek before rubbing her growing belly. We slipped outside, and we walked slowly down the driveway.

"Do you want to talk about it?" Julie asked.

I smiled over at her. "It's just hard to be back here. There was so much left unfinished."

She nodded but didn't say anything. Julie knew all about my time with Cara. She never judged me or her. Her fathers had a lot of friends who had a hard time dealing with their sexuality, and she always had a story that would help me understand what I was feeling.

"Love is love," she would say with a shrug as if it were all that simple. "A broken heart doesn't know what caused it to break. They all hurt the same."

"How did you get so wise?" I asked as I raise my eyebrow at her.

Her pale-blue eyes narrowed. She laughed. "I got my heart broken *a lot*."

We walked down Main Street, and as I saw Larson's Deli, I froze. Nostalgia washed over me, and I could almost taste the fries and milkshake.

"You want to go in there?" Julie asked as I looked over at her bright smile.

"You know what? No. Let's go back home." I grabbed Julie's hand, lacing our fingers as we headed back toward my father's house.

CHAPTER THIRTY
Cara

As I sat in Larson's Deli reading *The Good Girls* for the millionth time, I thought of Ellie as my eyes drifted over the e-reader. I would finally get to see her again today, and I was nervous that she wouldn't forgive me. If I was her, I probably wouldn't. The sound of a man clearing his throat pulled me from the story, and I was startled as I looked up to see Tristan. His face was clean-shaven, his hair cut a little shorter than the last time I'd seen him. I smiled nervously at him as his eyes narrowed. I think he was just as shocked to see me there as I was to see him.

"Tristan," I sputtered as I sat back in my seat. He nodded, running his palm over his eyebrow.

"It's been a long time." Shoving his hands in his pockets, he glanced down at the milkshake and fries on the table, his jaw clenched. "You here alone?" His haunted blue eyes met mine, and my heart sank. He wanted to know if I was here with Ellie.

"No…I mean yes, I'm here alone." Swallowing back the lump in my throat I gestured to the chair across from me but he only looked around the restaurant. I knew he was worried someone who knew what had happened was nearby. Guilt consumed me as I thought of the humiliation he'd endured. At the time I was so wrapped up in my own problems, I didn't consider how hard it had been on him.

"You?"

"Yeah. My mom is coming into town tomorrow."

"Do you want to talk?"

His eyes met mine as he thought that over. "Wanna go for a ride?"

I smiled, glad he wasn't hating me and grateful to have a distraction before going to see Ellie. I wanted to make sure I wouldn't intrude on Dawn's birthday party. I still wasn't sure how David and I would get along. "Sure. I'd like that." I shoved my new e-reader in my purse and took a sip of my soda before standing. I followed him out into the cool night as I waited for him to unlock the passenger door of his car and pull it open for me.

"Thanks," I slipped inside, my mind assaulted with the memories of the things we'd done in his car. It felt like another lifetime or a movie that I'd watched, not my actual memories. Tristan got in the driver's seat and began to drive, not saying a word. His body was tense, and I struggled to come up with the right words to help ease the tension. I wasn't the girl he'd known back then, and I hoped he'd understand and see that I'd changed.

"I never told you how sorry I was for everything that happened." I wrung my hands, inhaling a deep breath of air into my lungs. "I should have told you. I should have…said something." I paused, chancing a glance in his direction, but his eyes were fixed on the road, and he didn't say anything. I felt the need to fill the silence, so I continued. "If I could go back and do things differently, I would."

We turned off Shaffer Road and parked along a cornfield just off Huntington Road. I watched as his grip tightened on the steering wheel before he got out of the car and leaned against the front of it, facing away from me.

Pushing open my door, I walked toward him, hating myself for hurting someone I'd cared about. He gaze dropped to the ground between us as he crossed his arms over his chest.

"Brody told me he saw you kissing El at that first frat party. That true?"

My chest tightened, and all I could do was nod as I wiped my hand over my cheek to catch a stray tear.

"Is it true?"

I looked up at his narrowed eyes. "Yes," I whispered, thinking that the softness in my tone may somehow make the blow less harsh.

"You cheated on me? You used me the entire time she was here?"

"I did kiss her, but I didn't think it would mean anything. That's no excuse. I know that. But I wasn't using you, Tristan. I cared a lot about you."

He rubbed his hand over the back of his neck the way he did when he was stressed out about something. "You humiliated me in front of everyone. There isn't a goddamn person who doesn't know about it, and not a fucking day passes without it being thrown in my face because I wasn't man enough to keep you." He pushed from the car, standing so close now I had to look up at his face. "Was I not good enough for you? I fucking gave you everything, Cara."

"It didn't have anything to do with you."

"Bullshit. It had *everything* to do with me. I got hurt in this, too. Or do my feelings not fucking count?" His words echoed around the cavernous place causing me to turn to see if anyone could hear him, but we were completely alone.

"They do count, Tristan. They do. I just...I guess I thought I could change when I moved here—start over."

"Wait, you were a fucking dyke before we even started dating?" He bit out the words, and I flinched at the amount of anger in his voice. He stepped forward, and I took a step backward to avoid his chest colliding with mine.

"I loved you, Tris. It has nothing to do with being male or female." I held my palms toward him to keep him from getting closer, but he pressed against my hands, and I could feel his heart hammering in his chest.

"Oh, I think it does. I think it has everything to do with being a man." He pressed farther, and I took another step back, almost stumbling as my foot ended up in soil. "You want to be a fucking man, Cara?" He growled as his fingers wrapped around my wrists, gripping painfully tight. "You want to be a fucking man?" He yelled as he shoved me hard, sending me falling on my back, the wind knocked from my lungs. I gasped, desperate for air, my chest burning as he stood over me, a foot on each of my sides.

"Get up and fight like a fucking man, then."

I shook my head, tears flowing freely from my eyes and running into my hair as I finally was able to inhale. He grabbed my arms, yanking me from the cold ground, pulling me effortlessly to my feet.

"Please." A sob ripped from my throat as I tried to focus my blurred eyes on Tristan.

"Please? Please what, Cara?" he screamed, and it felt like my bones were going to snap under his grasp.

"Please don't hurt me."

He looked insulted as he looked me up and down. "Don't *hurt* you? What about you hurting *me*? What about that?"

"I'm so sorry, Tristan." My voice cracked as he readjusted his grip.

"You will be." His palm hit the side of my face before I'd even had time to register that he was swinging. The pain was like fire spreading over my cheek as I hit the ground, landing on my side because of the force of his blow. My mouth filled with the metallic taste of my own blood, and I could already feel my lip swelling. I rolled to my stomach and struggled to push myself up on my hands and knees as he grabbed my shoulder, shoving me onto my back.

"I'm a man, Cara, not you. I think you need a reminder of that."

I glanced up at him, my head throbbing and ears ringing. I watched as his hands fumbled with the buckle of his belt. I gagged as the blood from my lip ran back down my throat, and I turned my head to the side and coughed.

"Please," was all I could whisper, but my words were garbled. I felt the coldness of his fingertips on the waist of my jean shorts, and I pushed his hands away, but it only upset him more. He ripped my shorts down my legs, leaving claw marks in his wake as he tossed them out into the darkness.

My entire body shook as I cried, squeezing my eyes closed as tightly as possible as the weight of him pinned me to the ground. I wasn't strong enough to fight him off my body, but he couldn't control what was in my heart.

I dug my fingers into the soil, grasping at anything I could as I struggled to slip away into my imagination. I was the good girl from the novel, and Ellie was there with me, holding my hand. I hoped she'd never let me go.

CHAPTER THIRTY-ONE
Ellie

I stared out of my old bedroom window as my fingers played with the single pearl on my mother's necklace that hung from my neck. I'd stayed up the entire night, reading Cara's words in her novel that she'd left me. It was painful to go back to that time but also beautiful to hear how Cara thought about me in her own words. I needed to know that she'd loved me too. I felt like she'd finally given me the final piece of closure I needed to move forward. There was only one part of the story left unfinished.

David knocked, even though the door was open, and stepped inside. His hands were shoved deep in the pockets of his gray slacks, the top few buttons of his white shirt undone.

"It meant a lot to Dawn that you came this weekend."

I nodded, looking back out of the window so he wouldn't see written on my face how sad I was.

"I didn't think she'd show up."

"I did," I murmured to myself as a tear slipped over my lashes and fell on the window sill.

"Cara hasn't been back here since she left."

I rolled my eyes because I knew why she never returned.

"I'm going to head back to school tomorrow after I see Brody." I looked over at him now, and he nodded as he rubbed his hand over his jaw.

"It's hard to lose a friend, Elise. I know it was tough, because you'd confided in her after your mother passed away."

"She didn't pass away. She was murdered, and just because you don't say it, it doesn't mean it never happened. And Cara wasn't just a friend."

He frowned as he looked down at his brown loafers, struggling to find something to say to end the conversation. My father and I had grown closer after Cara left, but we were still far from perfect. I'd learned to accept that he was a man of few words.

"Will you be stopping back before you head out?"

"I'm not sure. I'll call you once I know what Brody and I will be doing."

He nodded once before stepping out of my room, pulling the door closed behind him.

"Dad," I called after him. The door popped back open, and he looked at me expectantly. "Why didn't you ever tell me why Cara was living with you?"

"She never told you?" He looked genuinely shocked and then relief washed over him. "Cara had an issue with an old friend of hers."

It hit me why he looked so relieved. He thought if Cara hadn't told me about a relationship in the past, we must not have been that close.

"What kind of issue?"

"The kind a lady should never have with another."

I knew I wasn't Cara's first because she'd slept with Tristan, but I never realized, until reading her book, that there had been another girl before me. That revelation was still too new to fully process.

"I know it's a lot to take in"—he shook his head in disappointment—"but it goes to show you that you never really know someone as well as you think you do."

My eyes met his as I struggled not to direct my anger toward him. He had no idea who his daughter was. He was happily oblivious.

"I know why she left."

He cleared his throat as he looked around the room.

"You made her leave because you thought she was too close to me."

"I was looking out for you, Ellie."

Julie came to the bedroom door when she heard my voice. "Everything okay?" she asked.

I nodded, wiping away a tear from my cheek. "You broke my heart, Dad." The tears fell now, and I didn't bother to try to hide them. I wanted him to understand what his hatred and fear had done. I glanced at Julie and felt the strength to continue on. If he didn't accept me, it would be okay, because I had other people who cared about me.

"She never told me why she had to go so I wouldn't be upset at you. Even after you sent her away and made her feel unwanted, she still made sure to keep your hatred a secret. Do you know why? Do you know *why* she let me blame her for disappearing all of this time?" I spoke with my jaw clenched as I struggled to keep my temper at bay. I wanted him to listen to what I was saying, and if his temper rose, he wouldn't fully grasp what I had to say to him. "Because she *loved* me…and I loved her."

My father's eyes widened before a single tear slid down his cheek.

I stalked across the room, grabbing my bag before slipping out of the door. I didn't give him a chance to respond, partly because I was scared of what he might say. But I also wanted to give him time to process what I'd told him so he could let it sink in.

I drove to the Hamilton Hotel just on the other side of town. Julie didn't say a word the entire trip, but she kept my hand in hers, letting me know I had someone to talk to when I was ready. My phone rang, and I turned off the sound. I needed some time.

I lay in the queen-size bed, staring at the ceiling. Julie's eyes were glued to my e-reader. I don't know what time sleep finally won over, but I didn't wake until ten the next morning. I groaned, grabbing my phone and seeing that I'd missed fourteen calls from my father. I knew he wanted to make amends before I left, but even I didn't expect him to put forth so much effort. Julie lay peacefully beside me, curled into a ball, facing the wall. I grabbed the blanket and pulled it over her and she groaned, snuggling into the warmth.

Slipping on my shoes, I left the room as quietly as possible and headed outside for some fresh air before I called David.

The phone only rang once, and when he answered he sounded like he hadn't slept at all.

"Ellie, where have you been? I've been trying to reach you for hours. It's Cara."

My heart sank at just the mention of her name. Had she finally come home to see me, and in my anger I'd left?

"She's there? I just need to wake Julie, and I can be there in a few minutes."

"No, Ellie, honey. Cara has had an accident. I'm over at Saint Vincent's Memorial."

The phone slipped from my hand and landed on the concrete beneath my feet, cracking simultaneously with my heart.

CHAPTER THIRTY-TWO
Cara

I woke up on a Tuesday. My eyes fluttered open, and I glanced around the stark white room. I was surrounded by paper swans that hung from the ceiling, and I held my breath, afraid that I hadn't survived my attack by Tristan. *Was this heaven? Had they somehow let me slip through?* The beeping of machines filled my ears, but a blurred vision of Ellie was what I struggled to focus on.

"I'm here," she spoke, and the beeping of my heart monitor increased as her fingers wrapped around mine.

I tried to speak, but my throat was raw and sore. A nurse was quickly by my side to give me a sip of water.

"Your throat was injured in the attack. Just take it easy," the nurse said as she placed her hand on my shoulder. I kept my eyes locked on El as if she was an illusion that would vanish if I looked away. *Please don't disappear.*

The nurse made a few notes on a clipboard and asked me a few questions before finally giving me a moment alone with Ellie. She leaned down, placing her forehead against mine, and I finally let my eyes close.

"We don't have much time," she whispered as she pulled back to look me in the eye. "This was Tristan, wasn't it? You have to tell them that this was a hate crime, Cara."

I shook my head as I croaked out the word no.

"You can't let him get away with this, Cara. I won't let you let him get away with this."

I shook my head again as she held up my cup of water so I could take another drink. "No one can know, El. Please. My mother…"

"Isn't a mother at all if she doesn't care about your safety or happiness."

"What happiness?" I asked, and she gave me a sad smile as her hand covered mine. My knuckles hurt, but I squeezed her back, needing to be closer to her.

"El, there aren't any laws in Georgia to prevent hate crimes."

I watched her lip quiver as that reality hit her. Our own government didn't accept us as equals.

"But he will still go to jail for what he's done."

"How much time do you think they'll give to a 'good ole' boy' who tried to cure me of my sins?"

Tears trailed down her cheeks as she silently cried.

My gaze drifted over Ellie's right shoulder to a girl with short red hair whose back was pressed against the wall. I looked back to Ellie, struggling to smile.

"Did you read my book?" I asked, the lump forming in my throat making it nearly impossible to talk now.

"Yes. Yes, I did." Her eyes glossed over, and I wanted to pull her in to hug me but my body felt so heavy. I glanced to the machine on my left and a long pole with bags hanging from it that were attached to my arm via tubes.

Ellie's gaze followed mine. "They have you on some good stuff, huh?"

I shrugged. "I've had better at some of those keg-gers." I smiled, and Ellie giggled, even though I knew she was struggling to remain serious. My smile faded. "Are you going to introduce me?"

Whatever Tristan had put me through, it was noth-ing to the pain in my chest at this moment. I'd already lost her. I could only hope that she was happy and didn't have to hide who she was any longer.

Ellie looked behind her before her eyes met mine. "That's Julie." The girl with the red hair stepped up beside Ellie and put her hand on her shoulder. In that moment, I wished I never had woken up. But I deserved every shard of glass pressed into my heart. I'd hurt Ellie, and I never would forgive myself for leaving her like I did.

"Are you all right?" Julie looked to Ellie. She swallowed hard and nodded. "I'm going to give you two a few minutes alone." She pressed a kiss to Ellie's temple, and I closed my eyes, not wanting to see the small token of affection.

I opened my eyes to find I was now alone with Ellie, who was struggling to hold herself together. I reached up with shaky fingers and slid the pad of my thumb under her eye, catching a tear.

"She's very beautiful," I said as I forced a smile. I didn't want her to feel guilty for moving on. As long as she was happy, I was happy for her.

"She is." Ellie glanced over her shoulder to the empty doorway. "Too bad she's straight."

"What?" I wasn't sure if the drugs had fogged my brain.

"As an arrow." Ellie laughed, shaking her head. She leaned in closer, and I held my breath as our eyes locked, her face turning serious. "But I *think* her two dads might be gay." Her eyebrow rose.

I laughed, pain shooting through my ribs. Ellie's smile faded as she placed her hand featherlight on my belly.

"I'm so sorry." She frowned, but I couldn't wipe the smile from my face.

"*I'm* sorry." I reached up, sliding my fingers into her silky hair. She leaned closer, pressing a soft kiss against my lips. "I love you so much."

"I love you, too, Cara. I always have."

"I wish you didn't."

Ellie pulled back from me, unable to hide the shock from her expression. She never was good at masking her feelings.

"I only mean that you wouldn't have gone through so much had I left you alone."

"Had you left me alone, I would have never known what it was like to truly love someone. It was worth all of the pain. *You* are worth it all."

"You would have found someone," I tucked her hair behind her ear, my eyes taking in her beauty. "I have no doubt in my mind."

"I don't want anyone else, Cara. What do I have to do to prove to you that I won't run away?"

I tried not to think of my mother or the others who'd left me behind when I needed them the most. Ellie was different.

"Marry me."

She laughed as she clasped her hand over her mouth and shook her head. "Okay, now I know they have you on some good drugs."

My eyes searched hers, and I had no doubt in my mind that she was the only person I wanted for the rest of my life.

"Not now, just promise me that this is forever."

Her smile faded when she realized I was serious; the gravity of the situation hit her. Leaning closer, she inhaled a ragged breath. Her gaze drifted to the ceiling, and I glanced up with her to look over the paper cranes that hung overhead.

"Is that your wish?" she asked as her eyes searched mine. I nodded as my hand slid to the back of her neck into her hair. I pulled her mouth to mine, wincing as pain shot through my swollen lip, but it was worth it. Every second of suffering was worth it to finally be able to call Ellie mine.

CHAPTER THIRTY-THREE
Ellie

Cara was released from the hospital, and she came to stay with David. I didn't return to school because I was terrified to leave her side. Instead, I gave my car to Julie so she wouldn't miss any classes. For two days, Cara would wince whenever she had to move, but she pretended that she was okay.

In the middle of the night, I'd wrap my arms and legs around her to keep her from hurting herself as she clawed at the sheets, engulfed in the memory of what Tristan had done. I felt helpless watching the person I loved struggling to overcome something so horrific. When she finally admitted, through broken sobs, how far the attack went, I couldn't breathe. It was as if he'd reached in my chest and squeezed the life from me. She never actually said the word rape, but she didn't have to. Part of me knew before she confessed. She refused to undress near me, and her body stiffened when hugged before she'd relax into me. Too much time had passed to even have enough evidence to prove he'd forced himself on her, and I was left feeling helpless.

It was killing me inside to see her suffer, and Tristan was going to walk away from it all. Cara didn't want our names dragged through the mud. In a small town like this, they wouldn't side with us. It was the reality of the situation, and it made me furious that I couldn't protect the person I loved.

By the fourth day of unbearable suffering, I called Brody, desperately in need to talk to someone.

He agreed to meet me while Cara was at her follow-up appointment with Dawn. Between her attack and coming out to our friends and family, I needed someone to confide in. I couldn't be strong any longer.

I waited on the steps of the library, lost in the pages of *On a Tuesday*, when his car pulled up to the curb. I stood, brushing off my bottom as he got out of the car and hurried toward me. His arms wrapped around my waist, and he lifted me from the bottom step in a tight hug before depositing me on the sidewalk.

"I've been worried about you two," he said as we walked to his car. I slid into the passenger seat and fiddled with the radio as he got in and buckled his seat belt.

"It's been a long couple of days, Bro." I shook my head, my eyes feeling like they were burned open from exhaustion.

"How is she feeling? Is she starting to heal?" He pulled out onto the road and began to slowly drive.

I glanced over at Brody's concerned expression and shook my head. The scars that Cara would wear from this attack were on the inside. "It's…so much worse than…it wasn't the beating that really hurt her…" I couldn't even finish my thought as I burst into tears. Brody pulled the car off the road and wrapped his strong arms around me, rubbing my back. I sobbed into his chest until my body felt like it had nothing left to give. I sagged against him as I tugged at the thin material of his T-shirt. It was the color of Cara's eyes, which were no longer vibrant and full of life.

Brody cleared his throat, causing his chest to rumble beneath my ear.

"He didn't," he whispered, shaking his head in disbelief as his arms banded around me tighter, crushing me in his grasp. "I'll fucking kill him, Ellie." His mouth was against my ear as he made me a quiet promise.

"You can't, Brody. Cara—" He cut me off before I could plead with him not to go after Tristan.

"I'm not asking for your permission." He pulled back and ran his hand over his face as the reality of what had happened hit him. "He did this to Ally."

"What?" I asked, lost in his train of thought.

"Ally, Tristan's ex."

The girl from the first frat party we attended flashed through my mind. "He…raped her?"

"He tried. She said he cornered her about a week after he got together with Cara. We all thought she was jealous. I'm going to be sick." His face paled as he leaned against the steering wheel, his head still shaking in disbelief. Brody put the car in drive and headed down the road in the direction of David's house.

"Where are we going?"

"I'm taking you home," he replied but wouldn't look at me.

"Why, Brody?" I watched as the muscles in his jaw ticked beneath his skin. I'd never seen him angry like this, and it was terrifying.

His eyes met mine briefly before he looked back to the road, stepping on the gas.

"Brody, Cara doesn't want this shared with the world. She doesn't want people to know what he did."

"Don't worry. He won't be able to talk with his fucking jaw wired shut." He turned down my driveway, kicking up stones in our path and leaving a cloud of dust in our wake. He stopped next to the front door and threw the car in park without saying a word.

"I'm not getting out."

Running his hand roughly over his hair, he struggled to calm his erratic breathing. "El, this is something I *have* to do."

I shook my head, begging my mind to come up with a logical reason that I could give him to make him reconsider, but I wanted Tristan to suffer for what he did as well. It made me sick to think that he'd turned us all into monsters just like him. "No."

He looked over at me, pain in his eyes.

"You think I don't want to hurt him? You think it isn't killing me inside that this prick hurt Cara, and I can't even defend her?"

"You don't have to."

"Brody, you can't fight our battles for us." I picked at the tattered frays on my jean shorts as my eyes blurred over with fresh tears.

"Someone needs to stand up for you, and if the fucking cops won't, I will."

"You'll go to jail."

"I'll put him in a fucking body bag first."

I looked over at Brody, my eyes wide with shock, but his expression was eerily calm. He had made up his mind, and I had to convince him not to.

"Have I ever told you...how much I love you?" I asked with a sad smile.

Brody's eyes glossed over. The column of his throat moved when he swallowed hard. He reached out, ghosting his knuckles over my cheek, and I leaned into his touch, the corners of my mouth tugging down in a frown.

"It's because of how much I love you that I have to do this." His eyebrows pulled together as if it physically pained him to say the words. "I hate to see you hurting."

I grabbed his hand from my face and pulled it to my lap, wrapping my fingers around his. "If anything happened to you, it would hurt me."

He looked down at our hands, and I ducked my head to catch his eye again. *"Please."*

"Ellie, I never lied to you." He pulled his hand free from mine as his expression turned hard again. "I won't start now."

I pressed the lock down on the passenger-side door and crossed my arms over my chest. "I won't leave you."

I was acting like a child, but I was at a complete loss as to what to do.

"Fine," he spat angrily as he put the car in drive and turned around, speeding back down the driveway. My heart was racing as we made our way across town toward Tristan's apartment. I knew without a doubt if we found him there, Brody would beat him within an inch of his life, and that was if he was lucky. I had my doubts that he would be able to stop once he got ahold of him. That only gave me a few minutes to stop this from happening and come up with something better.

I slammed my hands on the dash. Brody swerved and nearly ran off the road.

"His mom," I practically screamed. "His fucking mom." I began to laugh like an idiot.

Brody was looking at me as if I'd lost my mind. "Care to share with the rest of the class?"

I rolled my eyes but ignored his remark. "Tristan's mother is in town. Cara mentioned it as she told me…" I let my voice trail off and shook the vivid details from my mind. "His parents pay for everything, right?"

"Yeah, he's a spoiled fucking bitch."

"Exactly." I held up my hands as if the solution was obvious, but Brody still didn't seem to get it. "We tell his fucking mom. We show her what her precious son did to Cara."

"You can't just walk up to someone and tell them their son is a rapist."

I flinched at his words, and he placed his hand on my thigh and gave it a small squeeze before placing it back on the wheel.

"It's worth a shot, Bro. I want Tristan to pay for what he did to Cara, too, but not by you getting in trouble."

He sighed loudly and was quiet for a moment as he thought it over. When Tristan's apartment came into view, my heart seized in my chest. Brody threw the car into park and got out before I could even unbuckle my seat belt. I scrambled out of the car and hurried after him.

As he rang the doorbell, I glanced up at him. His gaze flicked to me, and he looked torn. I knew he didn't want to let Tristan get off so easily, and I was out of time.

As the door pulled open, I sighed with relief when it was one of his roommates.

"Where's Tris?" Brody had forgone any small talk, and I could almost feel the energy vibrating off him.

"How the fuck should I know?" the guy responded, his eyes glossed over and half-mast. I knew he was stoned, but with one look at Brody's narrowed gaze he seemed to sober up quickly. "I think he's with his mom. He said something about dinner." The guy gave an apologetic shrug, and Brody nodded once before turning and heading back to his car.

I jumped in the passenger seat and buckled quickly, afraid I'd get left behind if I didn't keep up with him. We took off down the road as my cell phone rang.

"Hey, baby. How was your appointment?" I asked as Cara sighed into the receiver.

"I never want to go to another doctor again."

"I wish I could have come along, but you know they would have made me wait outside because I'm not a relative."

"It's not fair," she mumbled, and I wished I could hold her.

"None of this is," I agreed as I looked to Brody.

"I should be home soon."

"Well, I...uh...I might not be there for a while."

"Why?" I could hear the panic in her voice. After the accident I'd barely left her side.

"I'm with Brody. We're at the library. I promise I won't be too late, okay?"

She was silent for a moment before she responded. "I miss you." Her voice sounded defeated.

"I miss you, too, Cara. I won't be long, okay?"

"I love you." She sounded so small, not the normal vibrant and fun-loving Cara she'd always been. But it warmed me to hear her say those words. I couldn't get enough of it.

"I love you, too."

We said our good-byes, and I cleared my throat, trying to push the sadness from my mind. I needed to keep focused on what was about to happen, because if I couldn't keep Brody away from Tristan, I might not make it back home to Cara tonight. The last thing anyone in our family needed was to have to visit me in jail.

"You lied to her," he said. He wasn't judging, but it still made my spine stiffen.

"I couldn't tell her we were going to go see Tris. It would kill her."

He nodded once but didn't respond as we continued down Main Street and turned off on Lincoln Road.

"That's his fucking car." Brody pulled off into a parking spot just two away from Tristan's vehicle and slammed the car into park.

CHAPTER THIRTY-FOUR

Cara

"I'm sure she'll be home soon," Dawn said as I clutched my phone in my hand, staring out of the passenger window.

"Do you think we can swing by the library?" I looked to Dawn with a pleading expression. I knew she was apprehensive about me being anywhere in town after what had happened. Fortunately, they didn't know the extent of what happened. "El is there with Brody, and I'd like to see him. I miss my friends."

She huffed out a breath, and I knew she was worried about what David would say, but she also didn't want to deny me after all I'd been through. She really did have a kind heart. "We can stop in for a few minutes. Have Brody come back to the house, and you guys can order pizza and watch some movies."

"Really?"

"Yeah. I think it would be good for you to have friends over, and Brody is a decent guy."

That made me laugh. A lot had changed since I'd been gone. That was the power of Ellie though. She changed everyone she touched with her life. "Thanks, Dawn."

We pulled up to the library a few minutes later, and I inched out of the car, glancing up and down the sidewalk as if Tristan was going to jump out from behind the bushes.

Dawn waited in the car, and I knew she was nervous about me going in alone, but I insisted she stay in the car; I wouldn't be long. I hated how everyone was treating me like I was breakable. It made me sick that Tristan had gained so much power over me.

I climbed the stairs, wincing as my ribs stabbed with pain. Grabbing the railing, I took each step slowly and used my arm to help pull me higher. As I reached the door, I stepped to the side as an older woman exited, smiling at her while she held the door for me because I was too weak.

I stepped inside as memories of the day I'd left Ellie washed over me. My eyes scanned the racks of books. There were a few scattered patrons, but the place was pretty much desolate. I wandered back toward the floor-to-ceiling shelving. With each empty row I passed, my heart began to pound rapidly in my chest. Panic settled into me, spreading throughout my veins.

I'd been getting attacks since the incident with Tristan, and it usually took Ellie cradling me in her arms to calm me down. But now the fear was caused by her absence, and it was killing me inside. I sank down to the floor and pulled my knees to my chest as I rocked slowly, crying into my knees.

A hand on my shoulder caused me to jump, releasing a yelp as I looked up to meet Dawn's gaze.

"It's just me," she said softly as she slid her hand under my arm and pulled me to my feet. "What happened?"

"Ellie." I looked down the aisle. "She's not here."

"It's okay. She probably went for ice cream or something. You know how she is." Dawn gave a small smile, but it did not ease the tension. "Come on. We can go check at Larson's Deli."

I yanked my arm free from her grasp and stumbled back into the shelf of books. "No. No, I don't want to go there," I was shaking my head back and forth, desperate to rid my mind of the horrible memories of that night with Tristan.

"Okay. It's okay. We can just call her. She is probably already back home, waiting for you."

Reluctantly I let her loop my arm around my back and guide me to the front door. The few people who were inside the library stared at me as if I had lost my mind.

When we stepped out into the warm Georgia air, I felt like I couldn't breathe, as if I was suffocating under the weight of what had happened. What if it was too much for Ellie? What if she left me for Brody? I couldn't blame her. Who would choose this life? Who would decide to be ostracized by the world and be forced to keep their love a secret? But I knew that just as I had no choice, neither did Ellie.

Still, I couldn't deny how important Brody was to her. He had held her up when I left her behind. As I climbed slowly into the car, I felt like what I had suffered only days ago would pale in comparison to what lay ahead.

We drove home in silence as I held my phone in my hand, too scared to call her. As we pulled down the long driveway, I noticed that Brody's car wasn't parked by the house. He could have dropped her off and left, knowing that I wasn't up for visitors yet. She was always thinking of me first, and here I was worried that she would just run away.

Dawn hurried to my side of the car and helped me from my seat. I waved her away and refused her help as I climbed the stairs to the front door. Once inside the quiet house, I began the arduous task of making it up to the second floor. I bypassed my bedroom, which I no longer used, and went straight for her door. I pushed it open, nearly crumbling when I looked over the unmade bed.

As I fought against the lump in my throat, I hit call on my phone, my heart fracturing with each unanswered ring.

I crossed the room and crawled into the bed, curling up with her pillow against my face to muffle my cries as I breathed in the faint scent of her.

As I drifted off to sleep the events of that horrible night assaulted me. I could feel the weight of Tristan's body on mine as I struggled to free myself from his grip. And as I did on that fateful night, I thought of Ellie to help me survive it. But her vision wouldn't come clearly, and soon it morphed into her and Brody.

I reached for her, begging her to free me from the pain as Brody took her in his arms and they drifted farther away from me.

Two hands gripped my shoulders, and I gasped for air, struggling to break their hold. As a scream ripped from my throat, my eyes opened, and my body stilled.

"It was just a dream. Shhh…" Ellie whispered as she pulled me against her chest. As I wrapped my arms around her, my eyes landed on Brody, and I released her, pushing her back from me.

"Where were you?" I asked accusingly.

"I'm so sorry I wasn't here for you when you slept." She tucked my hair behind my ear, and I swatted her hand away as my eyes narrowed at him.

"Where *were* you?" I asked through gritted teeth.

"We went to the library," El replied, glancing back at Brody before her eyes met mine. There was no emotion on her face, and I wanted to scream. I knew she was lying, and now she was doing it so effortlessly that had I not witnessed it myself, I'd have never known.

"Get out!" I shouted. El may have perfected her lying, but there was nothing but guilt on Brody's face. He was my friend. I knew he cared about Ellie, but he was my *friend*. I'd somehow managed to lose everyone who meant anything to me, and I'd never felt so alone in my life. Not even when I woke up in that field, my face turned up to the sun, my mind taking me to the day I'd walked through town with Ellie. The day she challenged me to stop caring about what others thought of me.

The only reason I forced myself to get to my feet and find help was because I couldn't put El through the pain of losing me that way. I had to see her one last time.

But now, looking her in the eye, I wished I had spared myself the suffering. Hot tears slicked my cheeks as I pushed my sweaty hair from my face. My entire body ached from tossing and turning. I grabbed a bottle of pills from the nightstand beside me, struggling with the childproof cap.

El reached for them, and I held them out of her reach. "Let me help you."

"I don't need your help," I growled as the lid popped free, sending pain killers flying and scattering across the bed. Sobbing in frustration I grabbed one and tossed it in my mouth before chugging half a bottle of water that I'd left there from last night.

I looked between the two of them as the anger built inside of me. I was so helpless and weak, and it was killing me.

"Why are you both still here?" I asked in the most even tone I could manage. "I told you to leave," I snapped. I looked directly at Ellie, who shrank back as if I'd physically assaulted her.

"Why are you being so mean to me?" Her voice was so small, she sounded like a child.

"Mean? You think *I'm* being mean to *you*?" I asked incredulously.

"Ellie," Brody said quietly, my attention snapping to him.

"Don't talk to her. Don't you dare come in here and try to soothe my cheating girlfriend."

His eyes narrowed before he took a step closer. "Ellie isn't…we're not…" But he was unable to form a coherent thought.

"Cara, it's not what you think." Ellie reached for my hand, and I pulled it back, wrapping my arms around myself. "You just have to trust me, okay?"

"Then what is it? Because you fucking lied to me! Now you ask me to trust you?" My voice rose as I tried to keep from breaking down again. Brody put his hand on Ellie's shoulder from behind her, and my eyes drifted over his busted knuckles.

I scanned her, petrified that he'd hurt her. I knew he'd never lay a finger on her but after what Tristan had done, I no longer felt safe around any man. *Tristan.* My eyes locked on Brody's as I sat up on my knees, swallowing hard against the fear of even speaking his name.

"You went after him?" My eyes fell to Ellie's. "You *saw* him? You went to see the fucking guy who nearly killed me?" My entire body was trembling. I was scared for her safety and felt betrayed by her going behind my back. I was going to be sick.

The medication began to take effect, surrounding my brain in a cloud. I looked back to Brody, and I wanted to knock his hand from her shoulder. "How could you take her near him after what he did to me? How could you put her safety in jeopardy like that?"

"She was never in any danger." He tried to reassure me, but I was blinded with anger as I watched his grip flex against her.

"He blames her for his humiliation. If this is what he'd do to a girl he supposedly loved, what do you think he'd do to Ellie?"

"He never had a chance," Brody bit out. I knew he didn't want to upset me. He really was a good guy, but he was refusing to back down. I looked at his busted hand again as I closed my eyes, shaking my head.

"One of you needs to tell me what happened."

"We never wanted to lie to you, Cara. I never thought you'd think..." His voice trailed off as he scratched the back of his head. "I would never hurt you like that. We were just scared to bring him up around you."

"So where were you really?"

"Brody didn't want Tristan to get away with what he did to you," Ellie said quietly as she tucked her hair behind her ear.

"You told him...everything?" I asked as my heart sank.

"Cara, I couldn't keep it in anymore. I've tried to be strong for you and to be what you need, but it was killing me inside."

I nodded, hating that she'd ever been put in that position. I didn't think of how hard it must have been for her during this time.

"It's okay. Come here." I pushed to my knees and reached for her, wrapping my arms around her neck and pulling her against my chest. Her arms slid around my sides, and she buried her face in the crook of my neck.

"Ellie didn't want any part of what happened, but I couldn't just let it go, Cara. He would have hurt someone else if someone didn't stop him." Brody sank down on the edge of the bed.

CHAPTER THIRTY-FIVE

Ellie

It felt incredible to be cradled in Cara's arms. It was torturous to have her upset at me. I couldn't believe that she'd think I'd ever betray her in that way, but we'd been through a lot over the course of our tumultuous relationship. I pulled back from her to look into her damp green eyes as I wiped away her tears with my thumbs.

"There is *nothing* I wouldn't do for you, Cara. I'd go into hell and fight the devil himself."

Her forehead fell against mine, and I could feel her cheeks pull up as she smiled. "It sounds like you did."

"Brody did most of the work." I almost laughed as I pulled back and looked over my shoulder to him.

"This isn't funny, El." Cara's face was wrought with concern, and it made my heart break. I'd tried to avoid all of this, but I'd be lying if I said I regretted it.

"You're right. I'm sorry."

Her anger dissipated, and she sighed as she leaned back against my headboard. "So tell me what happened." She wiped her hands over her cheeks as she grabbed my pillow, clutching it against her chest as if it would lessen the blows of our words.

"I'll be honest, I wanted to hurt him. I wanted to make him suffer every ounce as much as he'd made you," Brody said as Cara's gaze fell to the bed. I knew she was feeling guilty about her accusations. "We knew his mom was in town, so we went to find them. Ellie was completely against it."

His words earned me a small smile, and I couldn't help but get lost in her emerald gaze.

"We let his mother know what he'd done. She won't support him any longer. He's going to have to move to Chicago with his parents." I reached for her hand, and she let me pull it free from the pillow, looking hopeful.

"He's gone? He's going to leave?" Her eyes searched Brody's, and he nodded. A happy yelp escaped her as she lurched forward and wrapped her arms around me. As she pulled back, her brow furrowed in confusion. "Then what happened to your hands?"

I couldn't tell Cara the evil words he'd spewed as we told his transgressions to his mother. He'd tried to deny what he'd done, but when he ran out of excuses, his telltale temper got the best of him.

.With a sneer on his lips and ice in his veins, Tristan looked Brody in the eye and told him that he would make sure the same thing happened to me.

All hell broke loose. Brody was on Tristan as they both slammed into the ground. The growl that ripped from Brody's chest as his fists slammed into Tristan's face was absolutely terrifying.

Fortunately for Brody, most of the patrons had heard the disgusting things Tristan had said, and none were quick to step in and lend him a hand.

When the police eventually showed up, Brody and Tristan were immediately cuffed. I was sobbing as they pulled him through the doors of the restaurant and shoved him against a car to pat him down.

I stood on the sidewalk next to Tristan's mother as they were read their rights. Even as they were held by the cops, Tristan continued to run his mouth as blood poured from a wound in his lip.

He was screaming that he'd press charges, and Brody would suffer in prison for laying a hand on him. But as he continued to spew his bile, his mother stepped forward, holding up her hand to stop him from speaking.

"Violence is a disgusting act that plagues our communities." As she spoke, Tristan struggled to smile, proud that he was able to hide behind his mother's skirt. "I only wish that someone had come to *my* defense when I was alone at college and a boy thought he could take advantage of me."

Tristan's face fell as if he'd been hit again. "Mom?"

"We won't be pressing any charges." Her eyes locked on her son's. "You got exactly what you deserved. You should be thankful you weren't charged, because I doubt they would have been as merciful in prison."

After talking to the police, they were both eventually released. Tristan was terrified that the details behind the fight would be revealed.

"There was a small fight, but in the end he left with his mom," Brody explained, and Cara's shoulders fell as she relaxed.

"I don't know what to say," she whispered as I pulled her against my chest and pressed my lips to her forehead.

"Bro," she called out as she waved him to us. He crawled across the bed and wrapped his arms around the pair of us, crushing us under his arms.

"I don't know how I can thank you," Cara whispered as she pulled us both tighter against her.

"Threesome?" Brody pulled back, but not fast enough. Cara smacked him hard across the arm as he laughed uncontrollably.

"I love you, Brody. Don't push it," she warned as I grabbed us both, pulling us back in for another hug.

EPILOGUE
Cara

We got married on a Tuesday. The sun was warm, and the flowers were in bloom in Kissimmee, Florida. Ellie had insisted that we wait until after we'd graduated college to make our lifelong commitment. I didn't mind because I knew that we'd always be together. There was never a doubt in my mind after we found our way back into each other's lives.

I'd be lying if I said that it was an easy road from that point. Coming out officially to my parents didn't go as smoothly as I'd hoped. Even with me nearly being killed, they still couldn't find it in their hearts to forgive me. I had no other choice but to accept their decision not to be a part of my life.

David, however, had drastically changed his views when he realized how much hatred and bigotry had hurt his own daughter. When he witnessed how much Ellie had changed me, he knew that we were meant to be together, and no one had a right to tell us anything different.

As I sat in front of a gilded mirror and looked over my simple white gown, tears sprang to my eyes. Dawn was quick to wipe them away and scold me for nearly messing up my makeup. Aiden tugged at my veil. I picked him up, sitting him on my lap so he could see himself in the mirror. "You ready to be my ring bearer, with the help of your mommy, little one?"

Dawn looked at me with so much adoration it made my heart swell. "He's so handsome," I praised him, and she put her hand over her chest.

"Do you think one day you'll want a little one?"

"No," I said with a laugh as I shook my head. "It's too soon to talk about kids. Although I'd love to see a little one with Ellie's smile."

That comment caused Dawn to sigh as she lifted Aiden into her arms, propping him on her blue satin-covered hip.

"I'd be happy to help you all in that department," Brody called out from behind me. I caught his reflection in the mirror. He winked, and I narrowed my eyes.

"Keep your dirty hands off my wife," I warned as I pointed at his reflection. He held his hands in the air as if to surrender, and we both laughed. "Have you seen her?" I pulled my bottom lip between my teeth, dying to know how Ellie was holding up.

"For the millionth time." Brody stood and walked up behind me, placing his hands on my shoulders. I reached up and covered his fingers with mine. "She can't wait to see you in your dress. She is not going to run away. I promise." He placed a kiss on my cheek before patting my shoulder. "Now if you don't mind, she isn't your wife just yet, so I'm going to go pay her a visit." He waggled his eyebrows and jumped back as I swung my arm behind me.

"It's time," Dawn's voice shook with excitement. I rose from my chair, looking over myself one last time before following her to the door.

We got into place, my arm looped in Brody's as "Für Elise" by Beethoven began to play. We decided against the traditional wedding march because our marriage was anything but traditional. And I found the title appropriate because there was nothing I wouldn't do *for Elise*.

As I reached the end of the aisle I couldn't stop my knees from shaking. I turned to watch Ellie walk toward me, holding her father's arm. Her gown made her look like a princess with intricate lace and delicate pearls over the bodice. Her mother's single pearl hung from her neck, and her hair was pulled up in soft curls. Her eyes shimmered as recognition washed over her.

"This is the song," she whispered as I held her hands in mine. "All this time, this is what you've been humming."

I couldn't help but smile as I looked into the eyes of my future wife. "Für Elise."

She inhaled a sharp breath as she looked at me adoringly. "For Elise?"

"It's always been for you, Ellie. It always will be."

The End

ABOUT THE AUTHOR

I was a Russian spy at the ripe age of thirteen, given my uncanny ability to tell if someone was lying (I also read fortunes on the weekends). By sixteen I had become too much of a handful for the Lethal Intelligence Ensemble (LIE). I was quickly exiled to the South of France, where I worked with wayward elephants in the Circus of Roaming Animals and People (CRAP). I was able to make ends meet by selling my organs on the black market for pocket change and beer money. At the age of twenty-three, I decided to expand my horizons and become a blackjack dealer in Ireland. I loved the family atmosphere at Barney's Underground Liquor Lounge (BULL). People couldn't resist the allure of liquor up front and poker in the rear. Eventually I became tired of the rear and headed off to the United States to try my hand at tall tales. That is what brings us here today. If you have a moment I'd like to tell you a story.

(This bio is not to be taken seriously under any circumstances.)

The *New York Times* and *USA Today* best-selling author of the *White Trash Trilogy*, *The Note*, *Perfect Lie*, *Pretty Little Things*, the *Honor* series, *Safe Word*, and *Rellik*. www.TeresaMummert.com